DREAM FOR DANGER

Some of Tod's best friends were aliens, but they had been here forever. The other planets had heard of Earth's problem and had stopped sending settlers to live here. So Tod didn't expect to meet new aliens and never, never at the bottom of his own garden . . .

1609

ANNA LEWINS

Dream For Danger

A Magnet Book

First published in Great Britain 1987
by Blackie & Son Ltd.
This edition first published 1989
by Magnet Paperbacks
Michelin House, 81 Fulham Road, London SW3 6RB
Text copyright © 1987 Anna Lewins
Printed in Great Britain by
Cox & Wyman Ltd, Reading

ISBN 0 416 12832 7

CONTENTS

THE CONKER DOME

A dome had flattened the Barrett tool-shed. It must have fallen out of the sky without a sound and that was impossible. It meant aliens.

Tod peered out of his bedroom window at the poor shed. Half of it had vanished under the dome wall. Lumps of wood peppered the onion patch and broken spades made U-bends on the lawn. The dome just sat there, like a giant silver conker. Somewhere inside was old Hemlock House.

Some of Tod's best friends were aliens, but they had been here forever. The other planets had heard about Earth's problem and had stopped sending settlers to live here. Tod had never expected to meet new aliens and never, never at the bottom of his own garden.

Tod had weeded the vegetable garden yesterday afternoon. He had munched a few carrots and his dad had moaned about the poor crop. Now everything near the dome had gone daft-mad. Tomatoes the size of bucket-balls bulged out of the greenhouse door. The vegetable marrows were as big as donkeys.

Tod glanced down. About two dozen nids had gathered on the lawn. They were ignoring the food and that was the strangest thing of all.

It was Monday morning, three weeks before the Harvest Holiday, one week before his birthday. Tod decided to wear his special T-shirt. It had been bought new and 'A nid can run faster than a boy on a bicycle' printed on the front in red. That was a Barrett joke. Tod had once chased a nid from the top of the Hill to Food Street, peddling for dear life and never gaining. Only his mum would have put the joke on a T-shirt.

'Hey, Dad. Have you seen the Conker Dome? It's split the tool-shed in half and you should see the size of the tomatoes!'

'I have,' his dad said, gloomily. 'Great, ugly things. Who's going to buy tomatoes that size?'

Tod squinted out of the kitchen window. Nothing else had happened but the nids' red fur stood on end. Not much scared a nid, but something was worrying them. They looked as if they might vanish back into their holes at any moment. He was about to mention it when the City Hall siren started.

His dad groaned. 'I'm willing to bet half my lunch that's about the dome. It's bound to be trouble.' He shook his head. 'Trouble, trouble. Giant tomatoes in the garden. And what about my shed? I bet no one's going to buy me a new shed.'

Mrs Barrett and Tessa had coaxed the old video screen to life. It crackled a few times and Mr Barrett said 'Nids' teeth!', then the Chief of Alien Affairs grinned out at them. He was a Ragoth, like the head of dad's department at the Council, and his big nose twitched with excitement.

'Good morning, Friends and Visitors. This is Conrad Kroon of the Alien Affairs Office.'

One of the new aliens was sitting next to Mr Kroon. Tod was disappointed. It only had one head. Zoo looked more different and Tod had stopped noticing Zoo's funny face years ago.

Tessa nudged him. 'He's a bit blue.'

8

'Friends, I would like to introduce our Visitor from Scouros. This is Guardian Beryn.'

The Scouran nodded out of the screen and Tod saw what Tessa meant. Blue shone in the man's black hair and pale skin. Next to Mr Kroon's hairy, dog-nosed face, he looked cold and unfriendly.

'The Scourans are going to live on Hemlock Hill for a while.' The Chief suddenly looked worried and chewed one paw. 'I know you'll all welcome our Visitors but please don't go near their dome. Our new friends want to be left alone.'

Tod's mum leaned forwards and pinched him on the knee. 'That means you, Tod.'

The screen faded and Tod thought about the silver conker. He had already decided to be the first person inside. 'It is in our garden, Mum. I mean, it's trespassing . . .'

His dad waved a finger at him. 'No, Tod. You heard Mr Kroon. And I didn't like the look of that Scouran. He gave me Bad Feelings.'

Tessa caught Tod's eye and pulled a face at him. Their dad was always having Bad Feelings.

Tod liked his sister most of the time. She was the cleverest pupil in their year and shy about it, but she had once thumped Vinny Morgan for kicking a dog. She always helped Tod with his homework and he would have forgiven her anything for thumping Vinny Morgan.

Tod followed Tessa into her room. Her bed was already made and she had arranged her family of fur snurds along the pillow. The baby needed a good wash but it was so old it might come apart in the water. It had been new when their great-great-grandma was born. Tessa pressed her nose against the window. The conker dome sparkled, quietly.

'Come on, Tessa, we'll be late.'

'Everyone will have listened, so we'll all be late.'

She gnawed her lip for a few seconds. Then she shrugged. 'Mr Ku won't mind. Zoo can explain anything we miss.'

* * *

Hemlock Hill was the highest in New Capital and it had the best view. Tod balanced on the front gate and gazed over the City to the silver snail-trail of the River Thames. One day, he would row down-river into London, the Old Capital. It would take a long time because London was miles away to the east but he wanted to see it for himself. After all, every family in New Capital had once come from London.

Grandpa Turner was weeding his front garden, a red handkerchief on his head and his glasses held up with string. Tod yelled 'Good Morning', but his grandpa had forgotten to turn his hearing-aid on. Tessa waved to Mrs XXchai, then frowned at Tod to get off the gate. He ignored her. His eyes had found the big storehouses where all the leftovers were kept.

'Get off the gate, Tod. I can't get past.'

'In a minute.' He risked a downwards glance at the pavement. 'I'm getting used to being up high. I'm OK this far off the ground.'

Tessa sounded pleased. 'Aren't you dizzy?'

'Well—a bit. Hey, can you hear that . . . ?'

Tessa's hands were on the gate and she must have pushed it. Tod fell, squawking. But Tessa would never do a thing like that. The wind had blown him off.

Tessa screamed and landed next to him. Her school hat sailed into the hedge. Flat on the path, they heard the wind tear past the house and launch itself at the Conker Dome.

'Tod, what's happening?'

'I don't know!' He had to shout over the gale. 'I can hardly breathe!'

10

A news-sheet wrapped itself around Tod's head and he peeled it off. Leaves flew through the air, pieces of grass, whole branches. Tessa crossed her hands over her head and tried to curl into a ball. Their dad opened the front door and the wind turned him upside down. Tod saw the soles of his shoes and heard him yell 'Nids' teeth!'

The wind attacked the Hill. Deafened, Tod flinched up at the sky. Quite a long way up, just under the clouds, a swarm of grey insects flew towards the City Centre. Tod's mouth fell open. There was a horrible smell of cabbage.

The wind stopped. No insects. No cabbage. Not a sound, except for his dad yelling 'Nids' teeth!'

'You all right, Tessy?' Tod whispered.

She looked up at him. Grass knotted her hair and her brown eyes were frightened. She bit her lip and nodded. 'What do you think it was, Tod? Do you think it's because of the new aliens?'

'Snurks! I hope not!'

Tod and Tessa were twins—brown-eyed, dark-haired, sharp-chinned as fox cubs. Tod had a healthy crop of freckles; Tessa was pale and thin and, Tod had to admit, very plain. She was a small girl. He was even smaller, but he was the fastest boy in his class. He and Zoo chased nids to keep their speed up and they were going to enter the pairs' race at the next sports day.

Their dad ran down the path. 'Are you both all right?' He was so worried he forgot to moan. 'Tod, did you hurt yourself?'

Tod shook his head. 'No, I fell sort of slow. Dad, what was it? There was an awful pong of cabbage.'

They stood up and their mum came to straighten Tessa's skirt and knock the grass out of her hair.

Mr Barrett shook his head. He was thinking about the cabbage wind. 'Tod, I don't know about smelling

11

cabbage, but it feels as if the air's changed.' They all stood and sniffed. The air felt thundery. 'You mark my words, we'll wish those new aliens had never landed. So be careful!'

Now they were really late for school.

Tessa was quieter than usual but Tod had too much on his mind to worry. The new aliens had stolen part of the Barrett garden with their dome so it was only fair that he had a closer look at it. Tonight, maybe. Tessa was good and would make sure no one saw him. A Trimonese couple rattled past on a horse-cart and that made Tod think about Zoo. He looked forward to seeing Zoo.

Tessa pinched his arm. 'Tod, that man's watching us.'

A thin man in grey stared at them from the opposite side of the road. His eyes were as thick and yellow as egg-custard.

Tessa started to shiver. 'Don't look at him, Tod,' she whispered. 'He's bad.'

Telling Tod not to look at something was like putting a pear-cream tart in front of a nid and telling it not to eat it. He glared back at the thin man and watched the yellow eyes grow yellower and yellower.

Tod suddenly felt tired and his feet wanted to stop walking. It would be nice to rest for a while. He could sit down and go to sleep.

'Tod . . . ? Tod, what's wrong? Tod, keep walking!' Tessa dug her nails into his arm but he hardly felt it.

Tod's feet came to a dead stop and he blinked into the man's yellow eyes. His head hurt and his tongue jammed against his teeth. He was very cold. Somewhere far away, Tessa shouted at him and pinched his arm. Then he knew that the man was reading his mind.

Yellow eyes, his head thought. Custard. Conker

12

Dome. Apple trees. Apples and custard. The yellow eyes vacuum-cleaned the thoughts out of Tod's head. Nids on the lawn. Silver conker.

Tod tried to think. If he thought, maybe the yellow eyes would stop swallowing his loose memories. For a moment he could see again. It was odd. The man's skin was grey, not pink at all.

A voice pushed into Tod's head. He felt it squeeze under his brain and into his ears. 'Not yet,' it said. 'Wait for the Door to open. Then . . .' And it laughed.

Tessa put her hands over her eyes. Tod's knees folded and he grabbed her shoulder. All of his weight hit her and she staggered into the road.

'Can you smell it, Tessa? Cabbage . . . He must have come with the wind.'

The man had gone.

'Tod, what was he doing?'

Tessa looked scared and Tod made himself smile at her. His mouth felt frozen stiff. 'I think he was trying to read my mind. It's a good job you stopped me looking at him.'

'We should tell Dad as soon as we get home.'

Tod nodded and his head wobbled on his neck. It was the last time he was going to look at anyone with yellow eyes.

* * *

Zoo perched on the edge of his desk, chewing a pickled gurk. 'Hi there, Tod.' He grinned around the gurk. 'Just filling the stomachs.'

Zoo was Trimonese and so tall and fat that he needed a special chair, but he was the second-fastest runner in the class. All Trimonese were bald and their fluffy white eyebrows gave them strange, old-baby faces. Tod sometimes looked at Zoo and saw a milk-chocolate Easter egg on legs. Even his nails were milk-chocolate coloured.

'Hey, Zoo! Guess who's got Scourans at the bottom of the garden?'

Zoo stuffed the gurk into one of his cheek-pouches and craned forwards. 'I saw it on the video. What's their dome like? Is it big? Is it round or what? What colour is it? Do you think we could get inside?'

Tod grinned and backed away until Zoo stopped spurting questions. Box-brained Trimonese could never ask one thing at a time. He was used to it.

'It's like a giant silver conker. I'll tell you about it on Friday night.'

Zoo's baby face wrinkled in horror. 'I can't wait that long! Tod, don't be cruel! I'll explode if I have to wait!'

Tod sighed. 'All right. Open a brain-box and I'll tell you everything I can remember.'

It was a good morning. First geometry with Mr Ku, Zoo's dad, then biology and a chance to see if their snerd had produced pups. To Tod's delight, six blue-mouthed babies waddled around the tank in search of insects. They rolled into scaly balls if anyone talked too loudly, but they let Tessa tickle their bellies. The mother snerd honked and blew bubbles at them.

Morning break was all talk about the new aliens. Zoo and Tod crept away from the main yard and stretched out on the grass next to the stables. They both wanted to think and Zoo had two stomachs to fill. For Trimonese, eating always went with talking.

'Zoo?' Tod rested his chin in his hands. It might sound daft. 'Zoo, something really nasty happened this morning.'

'If you mean that wind, I know all about it. I've opened a new box for pongy hurricanes.' Another gurk appeared from the sack inside Zoo's overalls

14

and Tod felt in his own pocket for a chew-mint. Zoo looked at him. 'Or was there something else? You've been a bit quiet all morning.'

They had been friends for three years and Tod would have trusted Zoo as much as Tessa not to tell tales. He slithered closer and lowered his voice.

'I think something's happening. First the Conker Dome drops at the bottom of our garden, then we're all blown over, then . . . then there's this man with yellow eyes. He tried to read my mind.'

Zoo grunted. 'I bet he didn't find much to read.'

Tod grinned. Zoo still thought Earth-born kids were pretty stupid. If Zoo wanted to remember something, he thought up the right brain-box, opened it and searched inside until he found an answer. Trimonese had no word for 'forget'. Their heads were full of brain-boxes and the brain-boxes were full of everything they had ever heard or seen.

'I'm serious, Zoo. Didn't you smell cabbage in the wind? I could smell it when the man was there.'

Zoo patted his belly, happily. 'I like cabbage,' he said.

They were wrestling, bits of gurk and chew-mint flying, when a voice yelled their favourite word, 'Nids!!!' Two seconds later, four feet skidded on the grass towards the school kitchens.

Tod slid to a halt beside the kitchen door. Mr Pratt, their Headmaster, was already inside.

'Cook's sick of waiting an hour every time we call the Nid Squad. You're our best runners. It might be quicker if you chase the perishers instead. Come and see.'

The kitchens backed onto a grassy space dotted with nid-hills. Extractor fans usually stopped the steam escaping. If something spicy was cooking, the ancient machinery was not always powerful enough.

15

As soon as the smell of food reached fresh air, the grass would heave and out would pop the first nid.

No one knew how many nids there were on Earth. People though they had arrived on a Ragoth ship, liked what they saw and dug in. Tod knew that they lived in a maze of burrows, some for travelling, some for sleeping, some for nurseries for their nidlets. They could eat almost anything and that was the problem. They were always hungry. The Nid Squad fought a losing battle, chasing them from one stolen meal to the next.

'I once put a cream cake in the middle of the football pitch and set a stop-watch on it.' Mr Pratt shook his head. 'Forty-three nids in two minutes.'

'Twenty-one per minute, one every three seconds.' Zoo was impressed. 'That's a lot of nids.'

Then Tod gasped. 'Look! It's the queen nid!'

A good fifty nids had gathered outside the door. They sat on their back legs, tongues hanging out, and waited to see if anyone was going to feed them. If no one fed them, they would start to howl and fifty howling nids were not at all funny.

In the centre of the group was a larger, paler-red body. Her big front paws were already licked clean of soil and her small ears twitched, listening for running feet. Her white belly was so clean that Tod could see her stripy underbelly. Two bright-black beads of eyes peered straight at him.

'I've only seen her once before. She can really move.'

Mr Pratt nudged the door open and fifty bushy tails started to wag. Fifty flat noses sniffed and tongues of every length began to drip with greed.

'Now!'

Tod ran left, Zoo right, and nids scattered like ripples from a pair of angry pebbles. Except for the queen nid. Tod was so surprised, he nearly fell over her. Powerful hind legs caught him on the back of the shorts and he saw the long tongue roll. The queen nid grinned and blew him a raspberry. 'Pppppprrrrmpftt!' Then she ran and he chased her past the tennis courts, red in the face because Mr Pratt had seen a nid make a snerd out of him.

A high fence separated the sports field from the main road. Three strides away, Tod realized that he could not stop. The queen nid dug her back claws into the grass and soared skywards. Tod just did the same. He floated over the wooden planks. His breath came out in a 'Wheee!' of surprise. When he landed, there was a new nid-hill in the grass verge and no queen nid.

Mr Pratt told Tod to start training for the high jump as well as the pairs' race and Tod and Zoo grinned at each other. The high jump! Everyone in school knew Tod was petrified of heights.

* * *

It was an extra-special afternoon. One of the teachers had had a baby and the school visited her, class by class. Tod had only seen one baby before, a milk-chocolate Trimonese like Zoo. This one was a Ragoth, all black nose and closed eyes and soft, doggy ears. It was beautiful and Tessa talked about it all the way home. Fewer and fewer people could have babies and then they could only have one. No one knew why but it meant that there were fewer people every day. Mr Pratt said that Tod and Tessa were the only twins in the world.

Grandma Barrett had made her special vegetable soup with lots of tomatoes and the whole family tucked into a big dinner. There had been less home-work than usual and there was plenty of time to play with the rabbits and feed the goat. Later, Tod and Tessa stood next to the Conker Dome and gazed

17

at the sky between its long spikes. Each spike pointed to a star and the strange, silvery metal shivered when Tod touched it. Somehow, he had to get inside.

INSIDE THE DOME

Tuesday meant sports practice after school and pear-cream tart for dinner. Tod set off home at a jog and almost missed the girl on the wall. Her faint-blue skin stopped him.

'What are you staring at?'

She jumped down and Tod tried not to stare. It was difficult because she was so tall and her clothes were new. Four blue-black plaits hung down her back.

'I'm sorry. I didn't expect to see one of you outside.' Tod gulped. 'I mean, I thought you'd stay in the Conk . . . in your dome.'

'I'm not going to hide away in that thing.' She tossed her head, angrily. 'I wanted to come out, so I came out. And that's that. It's rude to stare.'

'I said I was sorry.' She had a ring on her left index finger that shone gold—except when it shone blue. Tod blinked. 'What's that ring made out of? It keeps changing colour.'

She laughed. 'It's blue gold. Don't you know anything, stupid?'

Tod's head shivered inside. All the day's thoughts muddled up and straightened out again. The girl slouched against the wall with her hands in her trouser pockets.

'You are stupid! I thought only babies were scared of heights, Tod Barrett.'

'You read my mind!'

She shrugged. 'It's quicker than asking a lot of questions. Anyway, I'm Luz Pelina Erath, but you'd better call me "Your Highness". You're only an ordinary boy.'

Tod could hardly speak. 'I'm not calling anyone "Your Highness" except the King and Queen! My dad said he didn't like Scourans. He was right. Go back to your own world, nid-eyes!'

The girl's face blued and her mouth twisted sideways. Tod knew she was doing something he would not like. He decided to make a dash for it. Then her eyes crossed and it was too late.

Tod's legs disappeared into the pavement. He looked down. Concrete, two round holes, a pair of bony knees . . . His feet, ankles, shins were all below the ground.

'Oh snurks!'

* * *

It took the firemen an hour to dig him out. Quite a crowd gathered, including Vinny Morgan, who was laughing, and Tod's dad, who was not. A newsteam appeared and Tod had to talk into a microphone and tell them about the girl with the blue anger. It was embarrassing.

'I knew this was going to happen. Trouble, trouble.' Mr Barrett stomped up the Hill. 'What next, that's what I'd like to know? We'll find the garden full of buried feet. You sure you're all right?'

Tod grunted. 'I'm mad, that's all. I hope they go back to Scouros.'

'I bet they don't, though.' His dad scowled. 'I bet you're on the Weekend News.'

Tod thought about being on the News. The whole

20

World would see him! Wow! And if everyone in the World knew what had happened to him, no one was going to blame him for sneaking into the dome. He started to whistle to himself.

* * *

After dinner Tod wandered into the garden. Birds twittered and the spicy tomato-leaf dust made him sneeze. And there was another sound. He slid between two conker-spikes and pressed an ear against the metal. Someone was riding a horse in there!

The ground heaved. It had to be a nid. The lawn split and Tod backed away. This was no nid, unless it was a giant one. It might be something else from the wind, another Yellow Eyes. He bent his knees and dropped into the grass.

A white paw scraped through the soil . . . and another. The ground crumbled around a grinning face with two red ears. Then the shoulders and body of a massive white dog forced through. With a last struggle and a sneeze, the dog bounded out of the hole. It looked pleased with itself and shook the length of its legs and tail in a shower of dirt. Three quick sniffs and it trotted off towards the road. Behind it was the new hole leading . . . Tod swallowed. He was sure the hole led into the dome.

The hole was wide enough to take two Tods but it led down and down into earth-smelling darkness. It might not be safe. Kids had dug tunnels and been buried alive before now. He would be daft-mad to go down there. Tod sighed, gave the broken ground a last kick and fell, feet first, into the hole.

Stony darkness, wet soil, sharp plant roots . . . Falling, bouncing . . . And a bump as he hit the bottom of the tunnel. Tod coughed and spat out a mouthful of dirt. Far above his head, in opposite directions, he could see two circles of light. Being Tod, he squirmed head-over-heels until he faced away from home and started to climb.

At first, he managed quite well and the light moved towards him. Then the floor started to rise, very steeply. Loose soil scattered down on him. A worm squidged under his knee. The next landslide crumbled right down his face and into his mouth. He swallowed soil and muddy tears ran down his neck.

Tod wondered if he was in serious trouble. He was wet through and shaking. Grit prickled his eyes and his fingers were raw. He had to rest. He would slide back down and find his breath. Just one last try. Tod threw his arm up, snatching for the edge of the hole, and a strong hand grabbed his wrist.

Tod yelled, the hand pulled, and he landed on the grass with a teeth-rattling thud.

'Hello, Tod Barrett.'

The first thing Tod saw was the horse. It was a machine, all metal ribs and levers. The second thing was the boy with the wicked grin and eyes like stars.

'I thought you'd get in here, sooner or later. My sister told me about you.' The boy's grin widened and Tod noticed the crooked little scar on his cheek.

'She started it!' Tod coughed and the alien boy patted him on the back until he could speak again. 'And she read my mind. She should have asked, first.'

'Luz never asks first. I'm Gilen Erath. I hope we'll be friends, even if we have flattened your father's tool-shed.'

The girl had read Tod's mind and she knew everything he knew. Now her brother knew everything as well. Tod looked at Gilen more closely. He liked the knee-high boots but the bright, new clothes looked a bit odd. And another thing!

'You're twins as well! I wish Zoo was here. He'd tell us the odds for two twins meeting two twins.'

'We always have twins on Scouros.' Then Gilen grinned and jumped to his feet. 'Do you want to ride Seth?'

Tod looked at the metal horse doubtfully. He liked small animals, like snerds. About to refuse, he saw a glitter of blue-gold in a line above Gilen's brows. When Gilen moved his head, it vanished.

'I'm sorry.' Tod said. 'I was staring again. That scar looks as if someone did it on purpose.'

'It's for luck.'

Tod thought about that. Scourans must be more alien than they looked. He did not know any other boys with a good-luck scar. 'How old are you, Gilen?'

The Scouran boy's eyes were river-ice coloured. They were full of light but they never blinked. 'Luz and I were born on the same day as you and your sister and your friend Zoo. We'll be twelve in a few days. Come and ride my horse.'

Later, Tod wondered if Gilen could put thoughts into other people's heads as well as taking them out. Suddenly, he wanted to ride the horse. Gilen pulled a metal rod from his belt and pointed it at the horse's head. Switches flipped open and the horse blew steam out of its nostrils. Inside it was a mass of curling plastic, flashing dials and tiny black boxes full of programs.

'I'm having trouble with your Earth gravity. Scouros is heavier.' Gilen shook his head. 'He's still a bit one-sided. Let me give you a leg up.'

Tod put his foot in the cupped hands and bounced into the saddle. He thought of something. 'I don't have to call you "Your Highness", do I, Gilen?'

All the blue ran out of his new friend's face. Gilen looked horrified. 'She is bad! Tell Luz not to say something and she always says it. She likes to show off.'

'You can say that again!' Tod was glad that Luz was safely out of his way. 'I suppose Guardian Beryn's your dad?'

'Our parents are both dead.' Gilen said it quietly but Tod felt a stab of sadness. 'I can't tell you about it, Tod. Now, hold on. Seth, trot!'

The horse's metal ears came forwards and it set off at a gentle trot. Tod bounced up and down and side to side, all at once. He started to giggle.

'Grip with your knees, Tod. Go up with the bounces. Let him throw you up.'

Curiosity bit into Tod like a nid into an apple. 'Gilen, why have you come to Earth? The other planets won't come near us any more. Don't you know what's happening here?'

Gilen whistled and Seth slowed to a walk. As far as Tod could see, the other boy was not even out of breath. His pale eyes frowned.

'I know what's happening, Tod, but I don't know why. There just aren't enough people to run your world any more. You spend hours growing your own food and you wear the same clothes your great-grandfathers wore. You have to repair old machines until they fall apart or hunt for spares. Your families are dying out.' Gilen sighed. 'It's as if something's trying to kill you all. I think it's very sad.'

'So does Tessa.'

The big horse stopped so Tod slid down onto the grass. Tessa would like Gilen; they both thought too much.

The Scouran boy laughed. 'Come on, Tod. Let's go and see Luz. If she's nasty, I'll sit on her.'

Gilen spun around and sprinted for the old house. Tod blinked at the thin boy's speed then gave a whoop of delight and raced after him.

Hemlock House had been empty for years. Overnight, the Scourans had repaired everything, even the glass in the greenhouse. Luz was inside the glass walls. To Tod's amazement, she was kneeling next to a huge pond, feeding insects to a honking crowd of snerds. Blue mouths opened in every direction and Luz tossed food into them. She never missed. Despite himself, Tod was impressed. Anyone who liked snerds had to be all right.

'Luz, Tod's come to see you. I'm going to go to school with him tomorrow.'

Tod discovered that he liked the idea.

Luz glared at him. 'That's stupid. All you have to do is read one of the teachers and you'll know it all anyway. Why do you want to sit with him every day?'

'It's better than sitting with you every day.' Gilen smiled at her and she pulled a face. 'Tod likes snerds, Luz, so he can't be all that bad.'

'I know he likes snerds. I still think it's stupid to be frightened of heights.'

'He's been riding Seth. That's quite high.'

Luz sniffed, then decided to give Tod a handful of insects to feed to the snerds. They were sitting, stroking the pups' soft scales, when Guardian Beryn appeared.

'The Wise Man would like to see you.'

Gilen nodded. 'I'll be with him in five minutes.'

Tod thought that the Guardian almost bowed. 'Of course.' He hesitated in the doorway. 'There were two more attempts to break into the dome last night. I thought you should know.'

'Thank you. I'll be careful.'

A thousand questions bubbled inside Tod's head. Before he could open his mouth, Gilen changed the subject.

'Tod. What do you want to do when you're older?

25

Be a Council man, like your father? Or a Storekeeper like your friend Mr Sweet?'

It was still strange when Gilen knew one of his secrets. Tod shrugged. 'I like the Stores. All of history's there, if you look for it. I've found clothes 300 years old. But the Earth might not have any people in another 300 years.'

Gilen was right, it was sad. No one spoke for a while and the snerds were happy to splash around with three friendly humans. Then Tod remembered what time it was.

'Gilen, I'd better go back before people start to worry. Thanks for the ride on Seth.'

They walked outside and Gilen thought a door in the dome wall. Tessa was on the other side, playing with the white dog.

Gilen stared at her. 'Baggash!' It sounded like a strong word. 'He isn't supposed to play with strangers, he's supposed to jump on them.'

Tod grinned. 'Tessa's always been good with animals.'

'She'd have to be good.' Gilen shook his head. 'Sheeni, you're a bad dog!'

The dog's red ears flattened to his head, guiltily. Tessa gazed at Luz in amazement. The Scouran girl was so pretty! Then she saw the metal horse and her eyes lit up. 'Oh Tod! Does it move?'

Luz laughed. 'Of course it moves. It wouldn't be much good if it didn't move, would it? I suppose you're this midget's sister?'

'He isn't a midget! And you're rude!'

Luz blued to the roots of her plaits and Gilen grabbed her. For a moment, they all shouted at once. Then Gilen yelled 'Shut up!' Tod had never shut up so fast in his life. Luz curled her nose and started to kick lumps of grass into the hole.

'Have you ever heard of the Scouran Firebirds,

Tessa?' Gilen smiled at her. 'They're part of our Great Legend. They steal fire for their feathers from the middle of the sun.'

Tessa shook her head. 'I would have remembered that.'

'Well, the first Firebirds were dull and brown, uglier than the ugliest of other birds. Then, one day, they heard that the sun was making a new planet. While the sun was busy helping the plants to grow, the Firebirds slipped into his fire and stole enough to turn their feathers into golden flames. That new planet was Scouros and the birds have lived in Scouran legend ever since.'

Gilen's hand closed on the air. When it opened, a yellow-gold flame licked along his palm.

'It's on fire!' Tod twisted around, trying to see a fire bucket, anything to put the flame out with. 'Gilen, roll on the floor! Put it out!'

'It won't burn me, Tod. Remember, it's a feather from a bird. That's all.'

Gilen held his hand out to Tessa and she made herself reach out to touch the feather. It *was* a feather! It felt like a feather, but it looked like a golden flame burning between her finger and thumb.

'Keep it for luck, Tessa.'

Luz scowled, angrily. 'All right, Gilen. If you like these two so much, we might as well tell them the key to the dome. It's "Kasha". Just say it or think it and the wall will open.'

Gilen swung around and Tod guessed that the key was only for Scourans. Now he and Tessa could come and go any time they used the word.

For a moment, the two Scourans just looked at each other. Then Gilen sighed. 'Tod, I'll meet you at your gate tomorrow morning. You can both come here any time you want but please ask me first. I don't want one of the Guardians to hurt you.'

27

When the dome had closed behind them, Tod patted Tessa on the head.

'What's that for?'

'For being brave in front of Luz.' He laughed. 'At least she won't be coming to school with us.'

Tessa gave him one of her thinking looks. She tucked the Firebird feather inside her blouse, then shook her head. 'I think she will. Not tomorrow, but I think she will.'

NIDS

The next morning Gilen waited for his new friends on the garden gate. To Tod's surpise he was wearing rather scruffy-looking overalls. They were white but most of the dazzle had faded out of them.

'These are the oldest clothes I could find.' Gilen prodded a piece of frayed cuff. 'I hope they're all right?'

Tessa smiled. 'Of course they're all right. Come on, we'll be late.'

The three friends set off down the hill, Tessa slightly in front, Gilen slightly behind and not looking very happy.

'Are you nervous?' Tod stared at him. 'You are, aren't you?'

'A bit. I've never been to a school before. I think I need a few days to get used to this world. Maybe it's the air. I don't feel as strong as I usually do.'

Tod glanced at Gilen's face. Without the faint-blue skin and the crooked scar, he could have been an Earth boy. A tired Earth boy.

'What's that noise?' Tessa stopped walking. 'Can you hear it? It's rumbling like Zoo's stomachs.'

The pavement shuddered under Tod's feet. He gave Gilen a 'What-do-you-think?' shrug and saw the silver eyes flash. He was half-way to asking a silly question when Gilen's arm whipped out and knocked Tessa backwards.

'Down, Tod!'

Gilen dived flat out and Tod followed. The metal grate missed Gilen's head by a centimetre. It hit the wall of the bicycle shop and brick dust and sharp chips of mortar scattered over Tod's legs.

'Don't get up!' Gilen rolled away. 'Tod, stay there.'

A manhole cover broke out of its hole and whistled across the road. Gilen waited until it was nearly on top of him, then threw himelf into the gutter. The cover smashed through a shop window. Glass rained down.

The bicycle took Gilen by surprise, flying straight at his legs. Tod heard the thud of handlebar on shin-bone. Gilen jumped at the pain, then gasped, choking.

'Oh no, don't breathe! They must be in the sewers!'

A horrible pong leaked out of the uncovered drains and slid downhill. Rotten eggs and rotten water and cabbage. Tod gurgled and grabbed his nose.

A puff of cement dust sent Gilen rolling sideways. The paving stones were crumbling. The whole pavement was cracking open. Three slabs tore free and there was no way they could miss him. Tessa screamed, 'Tod!'

Tod was up on his knees when the DIY shop exploded. Litre tins of paint whizzed over his head and he dived for cover. Splitting tins and breaking stones deafened him. Then silence.

Tod looked up. The road was covered in a rainbow blancmange of paint. Red swirled into green, pale blue speckled bright orange. Every tin had flattened to a metal saucer and the saucers stood in a neat pile against the shop wall. Gilen was dusting himself down. His white overalls were spotless.

'I've just painted the sewers. Don't worry, it's dry enough to touch.'

Tod put a finger on the multi-coloured mess. It was not even sticky. Paint was everywhere, except on their own bodies.

Gilen was watching him. 'Don't ask, Tod.'

Tod shook his head. 'I wouldn't know what to ask first, anyway.'

* * *

They were very late for school. There was no time to introduce Zoo to Gilen but Tod saw him open a new brain-box for Scourans. Zoo took one look at Gilen's thin hand and offered him a pickled gurk. Gilen grinned at him.

Miss Roberts' history lesson was a Tod favourite. The films of Old Britain fascinated him. He could not believe streets had ever been so crowded. Of course, as the films reached the 2400's, the streets stopped being crowded.

'Today, we're seeing one of the last films of Old Capital. It's dated May 2581, just months before the power died.' Miss Roberts tapped the top of the video until it coughed into action. 'If you remember, London was getting too big to run. Many people had moved to New Capital. The Royal Family stayed on, with the Government, but it was getting emptier every day.'

Tod watched the film move along the Thames, past the empty docklands and towards the Centre. He counted ten people, all of them older than his grandpa.

'When the electricity stopped working, everyone had to leave. They travelled up the river or used horse-carts or even pushed barrows. It must have been a terrible sight.'

The video showed a strange city of sky-scraping

31

office blocks next to old churches, shiny glass reflecting warm stone and alien metal. The Ragoth Temple in Old Capital had been one of the biggest in the world.

'What's that?' Gilen pointed to the grey shape beside the Houses of Parliament.

'It's the Grey Needle.' Zoo quickly opened brainbox 201.49. 'Three hundred point two-two metres high, fifty point seven metres around the base, grey metal all over with alien writing in black. No one's ever translated it.'

Gilen raised his hand. 'Please, Miss, where did the Needle come from?'

The film showed Heathrow Airport and the rows of strange 'airyplanes', all rusting away because there were too few people to want to fly them. Gilen widened his eyes and the video flickered and ran backwards. The whole class gasped.

The video man only came once a year. He said the warehouses were running out of spares. In a few years there would be no parts left for repairs, which would mean no more films. Even Vinny Morgan was careful with the video.

'If you don't mind, Gilen, I'll look after the machinery.' Miss Roberts sounded weak with shock. 'Who remembers the Grey Needle? You saw a film on it in the third year.'

Tessa raised her hand. 'I know someone built it about 600 years ago, Miss. You said it was to remind people of a war in another part of the galaxy.'

'The Century War.' Gilen frowned. 'That was when my . . . when my planet nearly changed leaders. The Hargs wanted Scouros. They pretended to be our friends, then attacked without warning and killed many people. They've got powers as well, but only to lie and cheat with. It took us a hundred years to chase them away.' He shook his head. 'I didn't think I'd see Harg metal here.'

The class looked at the Grey Needle. Tod thought it was ugly. Even the writing was ugly, like curled-up snakes and spiny beetles. When the video showed a close-up of the writing Tod saw Gilen read down a line.

'It doesn't make sense.' Gilen bit his lip. 'I wish I could see all of it. Who built it?'

'I think the Council built it . . .'

'They couldn't have, they'd have died. When you cut the metal it bleeds poison. Only the Hargs can touch it. They're so poisonous themselves it can't hurt them.'

After that, Gilen was very quiet. When the lesson ended, he touched Tod on the wrist. 'I'd like to see the Needle some time. Will you take me?'

The other kids slammed their desks and rushed outside. Tod's mind was on bucket-ball and he did not really listen. 'I suppose so. Come on, Zoo and I'll show you how to play b-ball.'

He had stood up when he saw the ice in the Scouran boy's eyes.

'Never mind, Tod. I can take myself.'

Zoo watched Gilen walk outside, then turned to look at Tod. 'It wouldn't be much use lying to him.' Then he grinned. 'I wish I could make the vid. run backwards like that. My dad would have a stomach attack!'

The bucket-ball was already on the move. It plopped through the bottomless bucket—a Rashid Yamani special—and Rashid was on the other team.

Tod quickly told Gilen the rules. No running holding the ball, no body-charging, always pass overhand and throw it in the bucket. Simple. Gilen shrugged and let Zoo push him into the middle of the yard.

33

Tod snatched the ball from Vinny and bounced it to Kelph, the Ragoth. Kelph trotted across the yard, barking with excitement. A large hand grabbed the ball back and Gilen just stood, still as a statue, in everyone's way.

'Run, Gilen!' Tod yelled. 'Get the ball!'

The silver eyes locked onto the ball. One moment Gilen was rooted to the ground, the next his arm shot out, grabbed the ball and threw it. It sailed into the bucket.

They started the next run, Zoo bouncing as high as the ball. As soon as anyone got within reach of Gilen, his arm snapped out and the ball plopped into the bucket.

'Gilen, run for it! Don't just stand there!' Tod felt cheated. He had wanted to teach Gilen to play. Instead, his friend had dead aim and he was so tall he made Tod feel like a dwarf.

Gilen started to run and it was impossible to get past him. He moved in sharp darts, turning so fast that bodies thudded together behind him. Every time he got the ball, no matter where he was standing, he just lobbed it into the bucket.

Tod lost his temper. This was no fun at all. 'You're supposed to pass it! Gilen, pass it to Marco!'

'He might miss.'

'That doesn't matter!' Gilen looked confused and Tod groaned. 'Look, it's a team game. Everyone has a chance to score.'

When Luz had been angry, she had turned a darker blue. Gilen's face darkened and his left hand suddenly jerked shut and burst the ball. He shoved the limp plastic into Tod's ribs. 'You play. It's a stupid game.'

Tod looked at the ruined bucket-ball, then at the rest of his team. He felt responsible. He was still thinking of something to say when Vinny Morgan barged past him and stood in Gilen's way.

'Hey, you've burst our ball! Say you're sorry, fish-eyes, or I'll burst your face for you.'

The yard gave an 'Oh-no' moan. Vinny had pestered everyone in his year. He enjoyed pushing people around more than playing bucket-ball and he did not like aliens.

'I said to say you're sorry, or I'll make you really blue. Black and blue!'

Gilen's colour faded back to normal and a wicked grin spread over his face. Tod knew that he was about to do something. Someone should warn Vinny. Someone should, but Tod wanted to know what Gilen was going to do. He kept his mouth shut and just rolled his eyes at Zoo.

'You're the school bully.' Gilen gave Vinny a once-over, head to big feet. 'It must be hard work being such a nid-mouth. Why don't you lie down and have a rest?'

Vinny opened his mouth, made a funny noise and sat on the yard. The next minute he was snoring.

'Nids!!'

Vinny rolled over and smiled in his sleep.

'Nids! By the tuck-shop!'

Two things happened at once. The bucket-ball blew back up and Gilen sprinted away faster than anything Tod had seen in his life.

One of the first-year girls had dropped a sugared frid. The yellow jelly had scarcely hit the grass when three nids shot out, rolling over each other to grab it. Seconds later the poor girl was surrounded by thirty nids. Their eyes peered at the odour-proof bag in her hand and their noses twitched at the sugar on her brown fingers. She looked terrified.

Gilen spun around the corner of the chemistry lab and slid to a halt. The red fur and beady black eyes reminded him of Scouran rock-squirrels. Tod's memory had been full of nids and Gilen guessed there was only one way to get rid of them.

'Throw the bag! Throw it as high as you can!'

The girl was too frightened to listen. Gilen changed his voice. 'Anita Gupta, throw the bag!'

Anita threw the bag into the air and the sky filled with jumping nids. Tod ran around the lab as Gilen launched himself. There was a loud howl and Gilen sprawled on the grass with a furious queen nid in his arms.

'He's caught a nid!'

The queen's fur spiked into a cactus flower. Her back legs attacked Gilen's ribs, a dozen kicks in a second. Gilen held on. Her digging paws clawed his arms and ripped his sleeves like razors. He just gritted his teeth. Finally, she stopped struggling and stuck her tongue out, watching him. Nid after nid popped out of the lawn. A sea of red fur and glittering eyes waited for the next move.

'A thousand and five nids.' Zoo whispered. 'And more coming. We'll have nids standing on our heads in a minute.'

Tod had been closer to nids than most people. He had heard them talking—something between water in a drain and breathy wheezing—and he had learnt to recognize their grassy, hamstery scent. He had once fallen over and a nid had bounced on his stomach. For a moment he had felt the fur on his bare arm and it had been so soft. Now nids of every age and size piled up on the grass.

Gilen loosened his grip and the queen nid slithered onto the grass. She shook herself and her bushy tail straightened. For a moment she looked as if she might race away. Instead, she started to gurgle and whiffle in nid-talk.

36

'She's talking to him!' Tod could hardly believe it. 'Zoo, she's talking to him!'

'I wonder what she's saying.'

Nids stood on nids. The pile slowly hid Gilen from view.

'Maybe they're eating him?' Tessa squeezed to the front of the crowd. 'Tod, can you see him?'

'No. Don't fret, Tessy. Nids never bite. If they wanted to eat us, we'd have gone years ago.'

Zoo nodded. 'Two hundred and seventy years ago. Look!'

The nids dived back down their burrows. In seconds all that was left was a lawn full of holes and the queen nid letting Gilen stroke her silky fur. Then she had gone as well.

Gilen walked back to them, rubbing his bruised ribs. The tears in his sleeves had blue splodges on them. Tod gulped. Gilen had blue blood!

'I'm sorry I lost my temper, Tod. I'm not much use at team games.'

He disappeared into the tuck-shop. When he came out, he gave Anita a new bag of frids. 'I'd better go and wake Vinny up, hadn't I?'

'No!' Tod groaned. 'No, I'll do it. I don't trust you, Gilen.'

Gilen grinned and followed Tod back to the yard. Everyone stared after them, speechless.

All Vinny could remember was that someone had made a snerd of him. He opened his eyes, saw Tod's face and jumped up. Then he made a big mistake. He grabbed Tod's shirt and aimed a punch at him.

'No!'

The ground shuddered and the air was suddenly full of electricity. Tod twisted to look at Gilen's eyes and they burned pure, terrifying, white. Then Vinny's fist opened and Tod sat down. Tiny blue-silver sparks crawled around Gilen's fingernails and

37

Vinny shot into the air like a fire-rocket. A loud splash and he was up to his neck in the biology pond, frightening the newts.

Vinny spluttered his way onto the grass. 'Nid-face!' he yelled, then saw Gilen's eyes and ran.

'Gilen, I don't think you should have done that.' Zoo frowned. 'You look terrible. All your blue's gone.'

'I know. I just couldn't help it.' Gilen rubbed one hand over his face and shivered. 'He won't do it again, Zoo.'

He was breathing too fast and Tessa touched his arm. 'Are you all right Gilen?'

Tessa looked at Gilen's pale face and knew she could not let him hurt so badly. She closed her eyes and wished the pain away.

Gilen's head flew up. 'Tessa . . . What did you do? The pain's gone.'

She blushed. 'I've always been able to do it, haven't I, Tod? I rub Mum's headaches better. You know you really frightened me for a minute. You wouldn't have really hurt Vinny, would you?'

Gilen shook his head. 'No. Anyone can hurt people, that's easy. I just wanted to frighten him.'

Tod choked. 'Well you frightened me, anyway! Putting him to sleep . . . And throwing him in the pond, like that . . .'

Gilen looked slightly embarrassed. 'I shouldn't have, but it's sometimes hard not to. It was funny . . .' His grin made Tod flinch. 'Anyway, he won't threaten you again. But I think I should leave him with something to remember . . . Just in case.'

Tod groaned. 'No Gilen! Oh snurks . . . Don't do anything else. Look, we've had enough for one day. Oh no, I know you've done something.'

Gilen just grinned. 'Wait and see,' he said.

* * *

38

Tod was very quiet on the walk home. He needed time to think. When they were level with the garden centre, he looked over the fence and let Gilen and Tessa walk on without him. Gilen had a way of avoiding questions about his home and family. Tod frowned and scratched the back of his head and saw Yellow Eyes on the other side of the road.

Yellow Eyes' face twisted with hatred and Tod breathed the horrible cabbage stink. Instinct made him jump forwards and put himself between Yellow Eyes and Gilen's unprotected back. It was like walking into a freezer.

Tod gasped. His bones felt nailed together with the cold and he could hardly breathe. Then a strange thing happened. The cabbage smell must have attracted a passing nid. The grass at the edge of the pavement lifted and a red nose poked out. Yellow Eyes jumped back, covering his face with his hands. He could not look at the bright little face. He turned and stumbled down a side-road and the nid blew him a raspberry.

Tod ran flat out until he caught the others. Gilen took one look at his face and wheeled around, his hand flying to his belt.

Gilen closed his eyes. 'Show yourself,' he said.

Tessa lifted both arms into the air. It looked snerd-brained. Tod was going to tell her so when he glanced up. His own arms were in the air. Doors opened up and down the street. People came out, silly looks on their faces, and stood with their arms in the air. A man with braces around his hips and shaving foam on his chin; a woman with a pan full of sausages; a policeman who had sneaked a quick pint and poured it over his helmet. Beer froth ran down the policeman's face. The people stared at each other and opened and closed their mouths without speaking. Gilen gazed over the crowd and everyone shivered when his eyes touched them.

'Too late, it's gone.' Gilen sighed and everyone snapped out of the trance. Some very angry people marched back to their houses. 'Are you all right, Tod?'

Tod forced himself to speak. His tongue was cold and flabby. 'It was Yellow Eyes, Tessa. He was staring at Gilen and his face was awful.' Gilen's hand moved away from his belt. 'Gilen, do you know who he is?'

'No.'

It was a lie. Tessa bit her lip and Tod choked, furious and hurt at the same time. He would never lie to Gilen and he had put his own body between Gilen and Yellow Eyes.

'All right then, have it your own way. But you can forget about coming to school with us, Gilen. I thought I liked you. Well, I don't. You aren't my friend. Just stay away from me.'

He grabbed Tessa's hand and pulled her away. They walked as fast as they could, not speaking or wanting to look at each other. The Council news-sheet blamed the flying manhole covers on gas in the sewers. Around the corner, the road was suddenly nid-red and orange, splodges of grassy green up the walls and a bicycle hanging from the top of a lamp-post. They stopped walking.

'Tod . . . ?'

'He shouldn't lie to us, Tessa.'

'I know.'

They glanced back. No sign of Gilen. Tessa pulled the Firebird feather out of her pocket and it still looked like a flame. Tod gazed at the painted road and the pieces of broken paving-stone. Very slowly, he started to walk down the hill again.

Gilen was on the grass outside the garden centre, his head on his knees, his arms covering his face.

Tod felt the anger trickle away. 'You OK, Gilen?'

The boy's head came up. His face was white and frightened. 'Why have you come back?'

'I don't know.' Tod dug his heels into the grass. 'We shouldn't have. You lied to us.'

'Tod, I had to. I can't tell you what's happening.' Gilen looked at Tessa, then back at Tod. 'If I did, you'd be in as much trouble as I am. I don't want to see you hurt.'

Tessa shook her head. 'We're your friends, Gilen. We should help each other.'

Tod stayed awake for a long time that night. Gilen was in trouble and Gilen was his friend. So, Tod had to help him. Simple, if he only knew what the trouble was. But, as sure as nids ate frids, something nasty was happening and Gilen was right in the middle.

THE DREAM-SELLER

Luz had decided that the dome was too boring. When Tod saw her, dark blue on the garden gate, he heaved a sigh. It was just what he needed.

'You don't look pleased to see me, Shorty.' Luz looked at him down her nose. 'Frightened I'll bury your feet again?'

Tod's ears burned. For the hundredth time, he was glad that Luz was Gilen's twin and not his.

Gilen groaned. 'Luz, don't start. You know what Brother Gyus said.'

'I know. "Do this, do that . . . !" I'm sick of being careful.' She kicked a stone over the road. 'I'm not frightened, even if you are. Come on, Tessa, let's leave these two scaredy-creeps alone.'

To Tod's surprise, Tessa grinned and nodded. The girls ran on ahead and their brothers exchanged pained glances before pelting down the Hill after them.

The Thursday market filled the square between Luther King Road and William Street. Tessa slowed to glance at the stalls and to pat the market people's horses. It must be wonderful to own a horse-cart. She had ridden Seth for an hour last night, and it was her idea of paradise.

Luz pretended to be bored but her eyes jumped from stall to stall. She had not bothered to remember everything in Tod's mind and the orange vegetables could have been lettuces, tomatoes or haddock. At least, she thought haddock was a vegetable.

'I wonder what he sells.' She pointed to a man whose stall looked almost empty. 'Let's go and ask him.'

It was ten to nine . . .

'Luz, we'll be late!'

Luz shrugged. 'So what?'

There was no point arguing with Luz. Tessa groaned and followed her.

The man hunched over his table, drawing patterns on a piece of cloth with a white chalk. Sunshine sizzled on the cotton awnings and the market people sweated and rolled their sleeves over their elbows. The man with the chalk was bundled into layers of coats and jackets and two or three pairs of patched trousers. A black felt hat flopped over his eyes and half-way down his bony nose. Tessa peered at his crooked mouth. It had no lips.

'What are you selling then?' Luz scowled at the white circles. 'Do you do pictures of people as well?'

'No, young lady. I sell dreams.'

Tessa's nose wrinkled, then she realized that she was smelling real cabbages. The next table was covered with vegetables and its Nid-Stop had worn off. A pile of brooms and several buckets of water were on hand in case a nid appeared.

'How can you sell dreams?' Luz moved closer and tried to see under the man's hat. 'A dream's a dream. You either have them or you don't.'

The man's mouth smiled. 'And you don't,' he said.

Tessa was startled. Was it true and, if it was, how did the man know?

Luz nodded. 'So how can you sell them? You can't put a dream in a bag and take it home with you.'

43

The man's smile grew. He started to draw patterns on a new cloth. Tessa saw dragons and flowers, ugly faces and flying birds. Each time she blinked, the chalk made different shapes. Luz was fascinated and the man slid the cloth between his fingers, teasing her.

'Now, this is a nice dream, just for you. Hold it when you go to sleep and it'll come slipping into your head. Do you want to buy, little lady?'

'No, she doesn't. We're both safer without dreams.'

Tessa jumped. She had not heard Gilen walk up behind her.

Luz stamped her foot. 'Gilen, I want to dream! Neither of us has had a good night's sleep since we got here.'

'Luz, stop it.'

Every face in the square turned and looked at Gilen. He had not raised his voice, but it had frozen anyone who heard it. Luz tossed her head, but she did not argue. She marched away and Tessa hurried after her.

The Dream-Seller smiled. 'They told me you were clever. But you won't always be there to look after the little lady.'

'Keep away from my sister.'

Gilen's face blued and he stood on the tips of his toes. Before Tod's astonished eyes, the stall's roof began to crumble. The cotton turned to powder and a gust of wind blew the whole thing into the Dream-Seller's face.

Behind the stall, a grassy hill separated the market from the church of St John the Baptist. Gilen stretched his fingers towards the church and Tod heard the dry crackle of power. A rainbow of light bounced off the stained-glass windows and hit the Dream-Seller's body like a laser. The man shrieked and leaped away in agony. His tongue was black and forked, like a snake's tongue.

'Yuk!' Tod stepped back into Gilen's legs. 'Gilen, his tongue! Yuk, yuk!'

'Come on. Don't look at his eyes, Tod.'

A week ago, Tod would have had to look at the man's eyes. Now he knew better. He spun around and raced down the street. When he reached the corner with School Road, he risked a quick glance back. The Dream-Seller stood behind his ruined stall with his fists clenched tight. Then there was a cracking, splintering groan and the church steeple slowly tied itself into a knot.

* * *

Zoo was impressed. 'Knotting steeples? That's something I'd like to see.'

'You're welcome.' Tod was still shaking. 'If you'd seen his tongue! Yuk, yuk! Snaky, globby thing. You know something, Zoo? I'm starting to get really scared.'

They had just finished cookery, Zoo's favourite lesson, and he was still too happy to take Tod seriously. Everyone was wondering why Vinny Morgan was so late for class.

'Well, I think someone's after Gilen.' Zoo sounded quite calm about it. 'We just find out who and why and then stop them. I don't suppose Gilen will tell us?'

Tod grinned. 'That would be too easy.'

* * *

They found out what Gilen had done to Vinny Morgan in geography. Vinny was late because it had taken him two hours to climb out of his garden.

'One million tins of baked beans!' Vinny looked stunned. 'There's tins of beans right up to the roof!'

45

Vinny had hurried straight to the class to see Gilen. 'You did it, didn't you?'

Gilen smiled. 'You're lucky I left them in the tins.'

They all thought of one million tins of raw baked beans.

Zoo whistled. 'That would fill his garden 5,000 feet deep!'

In the end, everyone laughed, even Vinny Morgan.

Tessa was still smiling about the beans at lunchtime when she realized that Luz had vanished. The Dream-Seller was at the school gate and Luz was taking something from him. A piece of cloth . . .

'Oh snurks!'

The man said something and laughed, then he saw Tessa's yellow sun-dress and his face shrivelled like a dried-out sponge. Tessa thought the Bad People hated colours, which was why they hated nids and why Gilen had poured paint down the sewers. The Dream-Seller hunched over and fled.

'Luz! Gilen said you shouldn't! That man's bad!'

'Don't be silly, Tessa. Dreams can't hurt.'

'How do you know?' Tessa asked, angrily. 'Gilen didn't trust him.'

'Gilen hasn't trusted anyone since our parents died.'

Of course, that was true. Tessa felt sad inside. 'Will he ever trust us?'

Luz shrugged. 'I think he wants to but he can't. There's a lot he doesn't want you to know. I think it would be better if you did.'

Tessa shook her head. 'If Gilen doesn't want us to know you mustn't tell us. He's very clever, so there must be a good reason.'

Luz glared at her and Tessa nearly ducked. 'I'm very clever too! And there is a reason. He's stupid.'

Guiltily, Tessa tried to calm the other girl down.

46

'Well, I suppose you know Gilen better than we do, Luz, but I'm getting really nervous. You know they attacked him, yesterday? They smashed windows . . . It was terrible.'

Luz had not known. Her face turned dark blue and she stamped her foot. 'He should have told me! I don't care if he doesn't trust you, but he'd better trust me or I'll thump him! Twins should tell each other everything!'

'Like you're going to tell him about that dream you've just bought?'

Luz looked smug. Tessa groaned and Luz smirked at her. 'I didn't buy a dream, clever-clever. I bought two dreams. One for Gilen, one for me. It will do us both good to have a rest with a nice dream.'

Tessa sighed and decided that Luz was impossible. As she walked back to the class, she thought she saw the Dream-Seller standing in the distance, smiling.

* * *

Tod woke up. Someone's elbow dug into his back. It was Friday night and Zoo had come to stay. He was cold and there was a pain in his ears.

'Zoo . . . ?'

Tod heard nothing. To be more truthful, he heard silence. His own voice was silent. Everything was silent. He hit Zoo as hard as he could. It should have made a slapping noise and Zoo should have yelled. Tod saw Zoo open his mouth and nothing came out. They stared at each other.

The door flew open and Tessa nearly fell inside.

This was it. Tod sprang out of bed and pointed to the window, mouthing 'Dome'. Zoo pulled his shoes on. The three friends raced down the stairs. There was no need to tiptoe. No one would have heard an elephant fall through the roof.

The dome seemed to be in one piece. Tod shouted

the opening word. Nothing happened. He shouted it again—no sound, no word, no door in the dome. Tessa closed her eyes and wrinkled her forehead and the door appeared. She had thought the word and thoughts did not have to make a noise.

Someone had locked Sheeni in his cage and Tod had no idea where the Guardians kept the key. He had never seen Sheeni locked up at all. Tod said a quick prayer and ran into the house.

The three friends sprinted upstairs, looking for Gilen's room. The first door opened on a sleeping Guardian. Zoo raced inside and picked the man up by the shoulders. The man stayed asleep even when Zoo slapped his face. Tod turned and ran for the next room. Another Guardian. Then the next.

Gilen was asleep, a scrap of material wrapped around his arm. Tod swallowed with relief and froze. A pale shape was growing out of the air next to Gilen's bed—a sort of crack, top, bottom, one side, a long hinge. A door.

Tessa had seen the door as well. The cracks widened and two pairs of feet started down invisible steps into the room. She recognized the Dream-Seller's patched trousers.

What to do? Zoo and Tod tried to talk to each other, made sign-language shapes, dashed to the side of the room to look for weapons. They needed help but there was no help. Just them. Everyone was asleep.

Tessa's brain clicked. She spun around and tore down the stairs, into the kitchen. She grabbed an armful of bottled fruit, then staggered outside, thinking 'Kasha' over and over again until the dome was full of holes. Then she smashed the bottles onto the grass.

Yellow Eyes raked his nails towards Gilen's face and the Dream-Seller knocked him backwards. For a

48

moment they stared at each other and hated each other. The Dream-Seller twisted his mouth into a pitying smile and Yellow Eyes shrank away.

The custard eyes turned and saw the two boys. Tod dropped the book he had been going to throw. What use was a book? He forgot what Gilen had said and looked at the Dream-Seller's eyes. Suddenly, he couldn't move and the Dream-Seller's black tongue laughed at him.

Tod wanted to cry. His throat hurt but he could not even cry. Zoo's fat body was frozen stiff, next to him. They watched the two men bend down and start to wrap Gilen in his sheets. They were taking him with them!

A new voice pushed into Tod's head. It hurt. When Gilen spoke to him, it was a friend's voice, a shared secret. This was different. It had broken into his head.

The Dream-Seller smiled. His eyes were empty, just holes with nothing inside. It was his voice inside Tod's head and it hissed with a thousand snakes. 'You're right, Tod Barrett. You'll never see your clever friend again. Our master wants to kill him himself.'

Tod's mind yelled, 'No!' There was no sound. No sound when the white dog launched itself across the room. No sound when its paws dug into Yellow Eyes's chest and threw him backwards.

The Dream-Seller screamed as a wave of nids swept through the door. Bright red fur flowed into the bedroom. Suddenly, Tessa was there, covered in fruit juice, her brown hair standing on end like a tooth-brush. She threw the last fruit bottle at the Dream-Seller. Purple juice and berries flooded down his neck. He was covered in zorberries and hungry nids tore at his layers of jacket.

Tod stumbled and fell into a soft pile of nids. He

49

breathed a mouthful of fur and sneezed and nids started to lick his face.

Yellow Eyes kicked and screamed up the invisible stairs. His clothes were bitten to rags. Underneath, his skin was hard and smooth, like an insect's shell.

The Dream-Seller staggered onto the stairs. His eyes hated looking at the red fur, but he was not running yet. Tod yelled and tried to get up. Nids stood on him and he slid down again.

The knife was grey, its blade hooked to tear into someone. The Dream-Seller scratched one of his sharp nails along the metal and beads of grey-green, glistening poison oozed out.

The queen nid leapt onto the bed and tore the scrap of material away from Gilen's arm then stuck her whiskers in his face. His eyes flew open. The knife was already falling for his heart.

The Scouran boy looked at the knife. He looked at the Dream-Seller. Then he lifted one hand and the sparks cracked brilliant blue over the bed. The knife jerked in mid-air and shattered. The pieces hissed like hot metal falling into water and vanished.

The Dream-Seller shook his fist once, then fled through the door. The next minute the thing had gone.

Nid-talk filled the room. Whiffling, gurgling, tongue-dripping nids.

'I let the nids in. They ate through the bars on Sheeni's cage.' Tessa tried to stand up but two dozen nids hung on to her pyjamas. 'Tod, I can hear myself again.'

Gilen fought his way out of the tangled sheets, muttering Scouran words and grating his teeth together. Sparks flickered around his fingers and up and down his bare feet. Then he saw the strip of cloth in the queen nid's mouth. It was the Dream-Seller's chalk drawing.

'Luz! I should have guessed! I dreamt about the Betrayer. I could see him and he was really there.' He closed his eyes 'I couldn't wake up. I just couldn't.'

There was no food left. The queen nid stretched herself and flicked her tail. Then she sprang over the crowded carpet and out of the door. A rush of red fur and there was not a nid in the place.

'You saved my life.' Gilen slid from the bed. 'How did you know?'

'We just knew,' Tod said.

Sheeni followed Gilen as closely as a dog could follow an angry boy. Every time Gilen changed direction, his claws skidded on the wooden floor, and he whined, afraid to lose sight of his master again. Gilen finally noticed. He stopped walking and stroked between the two red ears.

'Poor dog. I bet you were as frightened as I was.'

'Gilen!'

Luz skidded into the room and saw the end of a bad dream—broken glass and squashed berries on the floor; nid-prints half-way up the curtains; four people in pyjamas, Zoo with his shoes neatly laced underneath; Tessa covered in fruit juice; and the Dream-Seller's charm.

'It couldn't be that. They can't be that powerful.' Her lips trembled. 'I thought they had killed you.'

Gilen looked at his sister and all the things he was going to say seemed cruel. 'They nearly did but I can't yell at you. You're Luz, that's all. You can't help being Luz, you were just born like it. Someone betrayed us again. I just don't know what to do now. I can't think.'

His legs folded and he sat on the bed.

'But I can.' An old man stood in the doorway. 'I think I know why we had to come here.'

The old man bulged out of blue, striped pyjamas. This had to be Brother Gyus, the Wise Man.

51

'I wish I did.' Luz took a deep breath. 'You see, Gilen's our Prince. We came here because the Hargs were chasing us. Our father thought the Betrayer wanted to make peace with Scouros, then the Betrayer killed him. Gilen can't be King of Scouros until his brow-band shines. The Betrayer has to kill him before it does.'

'Gilen, you've got to trust your friends. I don't think the Betrayer can touch young minds as power-fully as he touches old ones.' Brother Gyus bent down to stroke Sheeni's ears. 'Now, all be quiet and I'll try to "see" what we should do.'

Tod sat on the floor with Tessa and Zoo listened with his round eyes very wide, brain-boxes flapping.

The old man muttered to himself in Scouran and in some older language. 'Five!' he said. 'Five fears and five powers. Cantora Lisha . . . Together. You're strong if you're together. Fight your deepest fears and find your powers, but only together.'

'Together!' Gilen shook his head. 'No,' he said.

Brother Gyus opened his eyes. 'Please, Gilen. Five is the Royal Number and this world has the number five over it. That's why we came here. The five is for the five of you, together. If you children fight your fears together you'll find great powers to help you. But now the Betrayer knows where you are. You have to leave New Capital tomorrow.'

'No. I'm going out alone.'

'If you do, you're dead.' The old eyes flashed, angrily. 'You can't do it on your own, child. You need your friends.'

Tod stood up. 'What do you mean? What powers? We can't go away, we're at school. I don't understand.'

'Tod, listen to me.' Brother Gyus patted his shoulder. 'No one will force you to help us. If you

52

do, you're risking your own life. But if you don't, I can't think of another world we can run to.'

'I won't run.' Gilen stood up and walked to the window. 'I won't run any more. If the Betrayer comes here, I'll wait for him and that will end it all.'

Zoo coughed and gave the old man a polite nod. His Easter-egg face was doubtful. 'Could you explain about these powers? I've never felt any powers that I can remember. I don't think I've got a deepest fear either.'

'You'll be as strong as fifty men, Zoo.'

Zoo said 'Oh,' and sat down.

The Wise One nodded. 'Luz already opens the ground around young boys' feet, and I think you've guessed your power, Tessa?'

Tessa nodded. 'I can heal people.'

'Your brother might find this more difficult to believe. Tod, you'll be able to fly.'

'Fly!?' Tod laughed, then stopped laughing and frowned instead. Fly? He was frightened of heights. That was a fear and a half if he was going to start flying. 'I don't believe you. I'm sorry, but that's snerd-brained. I'm as heavy as anyone else and I haven't got wings.'

'But you nearly floated over the school fence?' The old man nodded as Tod remembered. 'And Gilen . . .'

They all looked at Gilen. There was a hard, lonely look on his face and the Wise One shook his head. 'I think the Harg Leaders found out that you would be born, a long time ago. They knew you'd be the only one who could stop the Betrayer and they've been planning to kill you ever since. You've found some of your power but you're not strong enough to use it.'

Tod remembered the flying paint and Vinny Morgan and the policeman pouring beer over his own helmet. If this Betrayer was stronger than Gilen, Tod was not sure he wanted to meet him.

The Wise One looked worried. 'Gilen, you're a leader and your friends know it. When you tell someone to do something, they have to do it. You've got the future in your hands. He has to destroy you and he'll come here, himself, to do it.'

Gilen banged his fists on the window-sill. 'Then I'll go away on my own. I'll hide somewhere in the north where there aren't many people. I don't want anyone to be hurt because of me.'

'I wish it was that easy. He'll take over the whole universe unless he's stopped. Your friends can help you be strong enough to stop him. It's up to them whether they go with you.'

In the end, there was only one thing they could do. When Brother Gyus had finished speaking they all nodded. Gilen was their friend. They could not let him fight on his own.

SNOW IN SUMMER

Tod woke up in a strange, white light. He wondered if he was dreaming. For one thing, he was in a strange room with Zoo snoring beside him. Then the truth dawned. He jumped out of bed and ran to the window. Outside the world was covered with snow.

It was summer. Yesterday had been hot. Today they had snow.

'Zoo, wake up. It's snowed in the night. You won't believe it!'

'I'd believe anything after yesterday.' Zoo rolled out of bed and joined Tod at the window. He looked impressed. 'Thirteen-and-a-half centimetres since midnight. That's two-and-a-quarter centimetres an hour, if it's just stopped. Not bad for July.'

Two piles of winter clothes waited for them on the blanket-chest.

'Tod, are you scared, yet?'

'Not yet. How about you?'

Zoo laughed. 'Just hungry.'

Tod slithered into the soft inner clothes, then into the furry trousers and the padded jacket. The knee-high boots were quilted inside and had metal teeth on the soles to stop them slipping. There was a hood on the jacket and a fluffy hat to go underneath.

The whole outfit was snow-white, lined with bright orange.

Zoo approved. 'Wear it outside out for camouflage, inside out if you want the rest of us to find you.'

'And Yellow Eyes will love the orange!' Tod grinned. 'I feel like a snowman.'

Zoo patted his belly. 'I look like one. Tod! There's even a snack pocket, inside.'

Zoo tugged the pouch out of his jacket. It bulged with his favourite snack-bites. He took a mouthful and started to feel ten times better.

Tod pulled the white gloves on, then sighed. 'I can't help it, I keep remembering the Dream-Seller's eyes.'

Tessa and Luz were in the main hall, tucking into steaming bowls of oatmeal and honey. Tessa's hair was in four plaits and Tod guessed that Luz had helped her. Their clothes were white as well, but their hoods were trimmed with silver feathers that reflected the light like diamonds.

Zoo took a mouthful of the oatmeal mash and asked for the recipe. He filed it in brain-box 158.83a, beside oatcakes and porridge.

Brother Gyus had been talking about the Betrayer and the Hargs. 'Tessa asked me about the Dream-Seller and his yellow-eyed friend. They're Harg creatures, but they aren't alive like you four are alive. They're from the Betrayer's mind. He has the power to think thin air into a solid body, then make it fight for him. When his creatures are finished, they go back into his mind. The Betrayer is alive but he's a Harg Leader and that means he can't be hurt by metal or air or fire or water.'

Tessa put her spoon down. She looked worried. 'What happens if we meet him, then?'

The door opened and Gilen walked inside with

Sheeni. He must have heard because he was frowning. 'If we meet him, I've still got my father's throwdart. It isn't metal and it isn't fire so it might work, if I can say the words.'

Tod remembered Gilen's hand going to his belt when Yellow Eyes had threatened them. He had wondered why . . .

The Wise One gasped. 'Gilen! I thought you'd left that thing on Scouros. If you can't say the words, it'll lose its temper and turn on you, instead! You shouldn't even think about using it.'

Gilen shrugged and started on the oats. 'It's the only thing I've got left from my father. I couldn't leave it behind. Anyway, if I need it that badly, it won't matter if I forget the words.'

As soon as the bowls were empty, the Guardians brought five back packs and Brother Gyus opened them for a last-minute examination. They all had food and water, a compass-map, a groundsheet, a heat-pack and blankets. Tod had ropes and a toolkit; Zoo had an axe and a wind-break; Luz had a tiny stove and pans; Tessa had a chemical torch and the first-aid kit; and Gilen had specially bright flares and maps of the country.

The Wise One nodded. 'I hope nothing's missing. We worked on these all night. They're watertight, so they'll keep afloat if you fall in deep water and the light on top will glow when it gets wet . . . Remember, electricity doesn't work in the Old Capital.'

Tod glanced at Gilen and saw his eyes widen. Something about electricity had given him an idea and Tod wondered what it was.

'So . . . There we are.' Brother Gyus rubbed his nose and tried to smile. 'I suppose you'd better put them on.'

The room was crowded with Scourons watching

their Prince leave them. They might never see him again.

'We ask the Family Spirits to watch over you and the three moons of Scouros to give you their light. Your brow-band will shine, Gilen, I'm sure of it.' His voice shook and he had to stop. There were tears in his eyes. 'Our thoughts will be with you.'

Gilen turned around very fast, and led the way out into the snow.

* * *

The sky was so low Tod thought he could jump up and touch it. It was a grey lid on the world, like a dream or the video when the sound went off. Then he realized what was wrong. It was too quiet. The snow creaked under their boots but there was no other sound – no barking dogs, no birds twittering in the hedges. The Hill seemed to be asleep.

'It's a bit quiet for a Saturday morning.' Tod said. No one answered, so he got into stride with Gilen. 'Why snow?'

'To freeze the topsoil. It will stop the nids coming out.'

'Oh.' That was a new idea. Tod frowned. 'You mean the Betrayer's stopped them helping us?'

Gilen nodded and blew a long, white cloud. 'He won't make the same mistake twice. Tod, he's clever, don't forget that. He can lie and make people believe him . . . Sheeni, stop acting like a puppy!'

Sheeni had never seen snow before, and he bounded from drift to drift, rolling over and paddling his paws in the air. Some drifts were so deep that only the tip of his tail showed. He took big bites out of the snow and sneezed.

Gilen groaned. 'Look at him! I hope he's going to behave himself. He's too young to be a proper guard-dog.'

They walked past the market stalls and Tod pointed to the knot in the church steeple. 'If the Dream-Seller can do that to a steeple, what can he do to us?' He remembered the crunching sound of twisted wood and decided to change the subject. 'Gilan, can I see your throw-dart?'

Half of him expected Gilen to refuse. He was surprised when his friend pulled a thin piece of wood out of his jacket. It was pale yellow, one end pointed, the other with carved flights, like any ordinary dart.

'It doesn't look very dangerous. It isn't poisoned, is it?'

Gilen nearly choked. 'Scourans don't use poison! That's a coward's weapon.' Then he heard himself and winced. 'I'm sorry, Tod. No, it's a sound-powered weapon. Say the right words and it flies like a rocket. I don't know if I know them. My father never had time to teach me. I just hope the words are somewhere inside me and I can remember how to find them.'

'Will it really come after you if you get the words wrong?'

'You'd better believe it!' Gilen laughed. 'Throw-darts have got filthy tempers. It might stick me just for the fun of it.'

The dart slid back under his belt.

Zoo had been thinking. He approved of words, but not of words firing darts at people. Trimonese liked to talk things out reasonably. He tapped Gilen on the arm. 'Maybe we could talk it over with him.'

'Talk what over?' The silvery eyes were wide open, making Zoo squirm.

'Talk to the Betrayer and work something out.' It sounded silly.

'Don't you think we've tried that?'

'Well, I don't know. You can't have tried very hard or you wouldn't still be fighting.'

Gilen took a deep breath. Zoo saw him fight his temper. 'If we could work something out, we would have done it years ago.'

'I bet you didn't have the right negotiators.' Zoo stuck his chin out. 'I bet you didn't have Trimonese. I could talk to him for you.'

'Zoo, he doesn't want to talk.'

Not want to talk? That was like not wanting to eat. Zoo's mouth fell open. 'He must be a terrible man.'

After that, no one could think of anything else to say and Gilen was walking so fast. They all saved their breath and concentrated on keeping up with him.

A quarter of an hour slid by. The silence made Tod nervous. He twisted his head and saw Zoo mouthing, 'Where is everyone?' Tessa and Luz were strangely quiet. Only the dog gave the odd snort of enjoyment and nosed a lump of snow. Tod decided that enough was enough. He stopped walking.

'Gilen, can we talk? It's Saturday morning. There should be people everywhere.'

Gilen slowed down and finally stopped. 'All right. You want to know where we're going and where everyone else is?'

They nodded. Luz pointed to his face. 'And I want to know why you look so ill.'

'I'm not doing it on purpose, Luz. It's nice of you to worry.'

She snorted. 'Who's worried? I just don't want to have to carry you. The back pack's heavy enough.'

Zoo silently offered Gilen a gurk and Gilen laughed and shook his head. They all felt slightly better.

'All right, let's think about this.' Gilen looked at his watch. 'It's four minutes to eight. I want us to be as far away from here as possible by tonight. None of you have looked at the News Office clock, have you?'

None of them had.

'It's still on twelve. The Betrayer stopped the time. We were protected by the dome but everyone else is still at midnight. We'll be the only people moving except the Betrayer's hunters.'

They looked at the clock across the road. Both hands were on twelve.

'Anyway, that's why we're out on our own. Tod, you remember what the Wise One said about the electricity? It made me think about the history lesson. People had already been leaving the Old Capital because there weren't enough of them to run it. Then, one day, all the electrical equipment stopped working, even batteries. Can you imagine it? Suddenly, no power for the hospitals. No lifts in the office blocks. No pumps to push drinking water into people's homes. Everyone had to leave in a hurry and they came up-river to live in New Capital.'

Tod remembered. It was one of his favourite pieces of history.

'Well, I suddenly wondered why it had happened.' Gilen closed his eyes, for a moment. 'People had started having less children about six hundred years ago, which was when the Betrayer's family ran away from my family, after the Century War. Then, four hundred years later, one place in the whole world loses its electricity. Why?'

Tod's mouth had dried. He could see the lump in Zoo's cheek, where the gurk had been pushed into the cheek-pouch because Zoo could not swallow it.

Gilen's eyes opened. 'Why would he empty the Old Capital unless there's something there he doesn't want people to see? Maybe that something's stopping people having children. It might be stealing

61

people's strengh and giving it back to the Betrayer. If we can destroy it, maybe we can destroy him.'

Tod took a deep breath. 'And how are we going to destroy it?'

Gilen grinned. 'I'm working on it.' Then he was very serious, looking from one face to another. 'Whatever happens, I promise I won't let him hurt any of you. Now we have to hurry. We're going to the river.'

Bundled up in their new white clothes, the five friends felt comfortably warm and almost optimistic. They headed south, walking in the gutter to hide their tracks. The streets were white and empty and no one else had left footprints. It was as if the whole world had moved house in the night.

'There's always people rowing in the summer,' Tod remembered. 'All we have to do is find where the boats are moored. I think there's a place near the bridge. It's been a long time since I rowed a boat, though.'

Zoo had never rowed a boat. Gilen was more used to sailing ships on the Scouron Ocean, but he had raced the lifeboats against some of his friends. The two girls were willing to learn.

'We can all swim, can't we?' Gilen looked around and saw three nods. 'Tessa, can't you swim?'

Tessa blushed and looked at her boots. 'Not very well. Anyway, the back packs float, don't they?'

Gilen stopped walking and felt behind him at the shape of his pack.

'Know something? If these things floated, you'd be underneath the water. I think you'd have to put the emergency light on top and lie on it. I'm not sure they're such a good design.' He smiled at Tessa's worried face. 'I promise I'll be right beside you if you have to swim, Tessa.'

The River

It was a long walk. The snow dragged at their aching legs with every step. No one had the energy to talk. Once, at the end of a long stretch of road, Gilen looked back. Their footprints were black in the snow. Before Luz could stop him, he stretched his fingers and a breeze blew up the hill and wiped all the tracks away.

'Can you feel it? It's getting colder.' Gilen shivered. 'Everything will be frozen solid by tomorrow. He might freeze the river. We have to hurry.'

Tessa had never walked so far before. Her ankles throbbed and sweat trickled down her back. The other four strode ahead and she staggered into a trot to catch up with them again. Her legs were so short.

Tod stopped to wait for her. 'Come on, Tessa! Stop trolling about like a lame snerd.'

Gilen frowned at him. 'Tod, Tessa's right. We're going too fast. We won't be able to put up much of a fight if we're exhausted.'

Tessa felt her lips start to quiver. 'I'm sorry I'm so slow. I'm trying to walk faster . . .'

'I told you to join in at play-time.' Tod shook his head. 'You should have got yourself fit. Sewing won't be much good if Yellow Eyes jumps out on you.'

'Tod!' Tessa stared at him, horrified. 'That's cruel!'

It was cruel and unfair as well. She had been brave enough to thump Vinny, but Tod was suddenly frightened. What was he going to say to his mum and dad if Tessa was hurt? She might be killed.

Gilen's voice came into his head. 'Don't worry, Tod. I won't let anyone hurt Tessa. I'll die first.'

Their eyes met, Tod's brown and Gilen's silvery-green. Tod blinked and looked away and thought a 'thank you'. Out of the corner of his eye, he saw Gilen say something to Sheeni. After that, the big dog stayed next to Tessa and wagged his tail and nuzzled her wrist above her glove. It was Gilen's way of making her happy again.

* * *

They were on Bridge Road, almost at the river bank, when the grey men appeared. Sheeni stiffened and sniffed. Then his red ears folded to his head and he started to growl in the deepest part of his throat.

A hundred metres to the wooden landing stage and two dozen rowing boats.

No one had wanted to stop for dinner. They were hungry and tired. Darkness touched the snow with blue and grey shadows. Then three of the shadows were men, running out of the horse-bus shelter. Tall, thin men with legs longer than any legs Tod had ever seen. They had two knees on each leg and their strides were four metres long.

'Girls, run! Get a boat, cut the others free!' Gilen twisted around. 'Sheeni, hunt!'

Tod's teeth snapped together as the dog snarled and threw itself at the men. The first man sprawled backwards taking the second man with him. The third ran on and his face was grey iron, the eyes glittering clusters of black beads, like a fly's eyes. Tod counted the steps the man would take to be in range. Ten . . . Nine . . .

64

Tod dodged right, Gilen left and the grey man skidded between them. While he was still off balance, Zoo spun on his tiny feet, threw out a fist and knocked him flat.

Gilen laughed. 'Team-work!' Then, not laughing, 'Tod! Leap-frog!!'

Tod doubled up, hands on knees, and a crashing weight hit him on the back. The air spluttered out of his lungs but he straightened his legs and sent the thin body flying. Gilen pounced, knees first, on the fallen grey man's stomach. It sounded like squashed tomatoes. The man squealed.

The other men pulled themselves up. One kicked and punched at Sheeni, trying to get some hold on the white fur. The second ran at Zoo, arms outstretched. Zoo grinned, stuck his belly out and bounced the grey body back into the snow.

'Come on! Tod, Gilen!' Luz screamed at them. 'Come on, we've got a boat!'

Gilen looked up. 'Run,' he said.

They were all fast runners, three boys and a dog, but the grey men almost caught them. Their long legs were made for hunting smaller animals down. Gilen reached the river bank first. He slid and nearly fell into the water. Back up the road, the grey men were gaining. His eyes narrowed and he spread both hands to point at the grey runners. Blue sparked between his fingers and the long legs suddenly ran in slow motion.

Still too fast. Gilen saw a grey hand claw towards Tod's jacket. Luz had cast off and the boat was pulling out into the dark water. They needed to jump now, or it would be gone. Zoo flew past, knees bent for the impact. Then Sheeni, yelping with excitement.

'Tod, jump now!'

It was a long way. Tod was panting, his hat

slipping over his nose, but he suddenly had to look into Gilen's river-ice eyes. They were silver mirrors and he could see the grey hand reflected inside them, closing on his hood. He yelled and jumped. Gilen jumped after him. They landed in the middle of the boat, bruising their legs and elbows on the wooden seat. For a moment the boat was dangerously broadside to the river. Luz groaned and dug an oar into the weight of water. And they were away, sliding into the middle of the current.

The boat shot under the smallest arch of the bridge and Gilen accidentally knelt on Tod's fingers, climbing over him to grab another oar. Poor bones! Tod heard them crunch under the skin. There was no time to yell.

No one spoke for five minutes as they tried to avoid the small island in the middle of the river. The girls had taken the biggest boat and it had a rudder, but Tessa could hardly keep it still. Zoo scrambled next to her and his weight was too far to the side. The boat tipped and water sloshed over the oar locks. Tod dived in the opposite direction and they were balanced again.

Gilen managed to speak. 'Now they know which way we're going. It's a pity, we could have done with a head start.'

It was time to rest. Tod sucked the cold air into his lungs and wondered what was going to happen next. Excitement had kept him warm. He knew that his knees were sore and his poor fingers felt squelched to a pulp, but his fear had vanished when Gilen had laughed.

'Well, we haven't been down the river before.' Gilen seemed quite cheerful. Sheeni stretched out and put both paws in his lap. 'According to the map—Sheeni, get your paws off the map!—there's a long way to go and a lot of bridges and it's starting

66

to get dark. Our best hope's to follow the river for as long as we can and leave the boat before morning. If it's a dark night, they won't see us but we won't see them either.'

Tod gazed back towards New Capital. The street lamps had been on all day. Now hundreds of points of light glittered against the snow.

Zoo coughed. 'Can I ask something, Gilen?'

'Of course you can. We aren't at school any more.'

'I know we aren't. It's just a bit hard to believe we're really doing this.' Zoo pointed to the river. 'If you'd told me I'd be running away from home through snow, in summer, sitting in a rowing boat. Well, you know what I mean. I just wondered. Can we eat, now?'

His stomachs rumbled and everyone started to laugh.

They took turns to munch on fruit loaf and potato crunch. They were ravenous and food had never tasted better. Tod glanced up and saw Gilen catch a handful of river water and whisper Scouran words over it. He nudged Luz with his foot and she scowled at him, then saw what Gilen was doing. Her face looked odd, as if she wasn't sure whether to laugh or be serious. She moved closer.

'He's thanking the River Spirits for looking after us.' She whispered. 'There's Drasha for the deep water and Shalty for the shallows and Old Earth-Head for the mud at the bottom. Gilen believes in that sort of thing.'

'Don't you?'

Luz snorted scornfully, but her dark eyes were nervous. 'Of course not. It's just superstition. He gets it from talking to animals all the time. Animals are really superstitious. Except for cats.'

Night fell swiftly. They soon had to travel by the

sound of the river. There was no moon and no man-made light onshore. Luckily, the white of the snow traced the river bank.

They had launched the boat through the third bridge, nearly deafened by the noise, when Tessa slid to take Gilen's place at the starboard oar. They were working a rota, two people to steer, two to row, one resting. The air crackled with bitter cold. Everyone had pulled their hats down as far as possible and fastened their hoods tight. The girls had tied their plaits around their necks like scarves. Steam curled out of the tops of their collars and their breath was smoke in front of their noses.

'Gilen, we're going faster, aren't we? That bridge was much louder and it's harder to hold the rudder straight.'

'Yes, the current's getting stronger all the time,' he admitted. Everyone listened, suddenly sitting very still. 'There's another bridge and then a long bend towards the centre of Old Capital. Then we start getting bridges closer and closer together. We need Westminster Bridge.'

Gilen let his hand drop into the water for a moment, and tore it out with a yell. 'It's colder than freezing!'

Zoo stared at him. 'That's impossible. If it was below freezing, it'd be frozen.' Then he frowned and hurriedly opened a brain-box. 'Wouldn't it?'

Gilen shook his head. 'It's unnatural, but not impossible. Not if you have powers, and the Betrayer has great powers. Don't forget that, Zoo. No one knows just how powerful he is . . .' He stopped and looked away.

The river was very straight. Tod tried to move the rudder just a centimetre to the left. It was like pulling against a locked door. The dark roofs of buildings blurred past. And something else.

'Gilen, bridge ahead!'

'Already?' Everyone craned forwards and saw the darker hole in the darkness. Gilen studied the map. 'Zoo, there's about one point six miles between those bridges.'

Zoo's mind whirred in calculation. He gasped. 'Then we're doing ten land-miles an hour. And getting faster by the feel of it.'

Gilen's eyes came wide open. 'I know what he's doing! Zoo, take the rudder with Tod. Tessa, Luz, both take the other oar. We've got to get ashore, now. He's trying to take us right through the City without stopping. We'll be in open sea by the morning at this speed.' He gritted his teeth. 'That means I was right. There must be something in the City he daren't let us find. Come on, pull together!'

They tried but it was already too late. They roared under the bridge, one mile to go before the next set of arches. After five minutes of straining to turn the boat they were under that bridge as well, heading north towards the City. The night had turned black around them and the boat had a life of its own. Cold spray rained down and the fur and feathers of their hoods dripped onto their faces. Their lips were so cold, words came out muffled and stupid.

The force of the water had started to carve great bites of snow and mud away from the river banks. Branches and frozen plants covered the water and scratched against the boat's prow. The current was fierce. They all saw the next obstacles coming—two bridges close together. Tod and Zoo strained on the rudder but the current was too strong. The boat side-swiped one of the concrete piers and its wooden planks split. An oar almost fell overboard and Tessa squealed trying to keep hold of it. Water started to ooze in and Luz did emergency repair work, thinking the crack closed.

Silence. Tessa was too shaken to speak. Tod and Zoo clung to the rudder and exchanged frightened glances. Luz finally forced her lips to move.

'Well, Gilen. We're in trouble, aren't we? What are we going to do?' She sounded angry. In the darkness it was hard to tell. 'We're just about finished. I could hardly fix that tiny crack I'm so tired '

'We could run all the way to Scotland, if you want.' Gilen kicked the side of the boat and Sheeni yelped. 'He'd still come after us. Do you want the Hargs to win because we're too scared to fight them?'

No one answered. They all moved away from each other and concentrated on keeping their strength.

The silence stretched on. They were all rowing machines, hearing an approaching bridge, tensing on oars and rudder, fighting to keep the boat away from the arches. It was pitch-black, below freezing, and everyone ached with cramped muscles when Gilen pointed ahead.

'That's Westminster Bridge. We must be passing the Houses of Parliament. It's as if . . . Luz, what do you feel?'

No one breathed. They stared at the left bank of the river. There was a darker shape of old buildings against the sky. As they drew level, Luz shuddered.

'I feel horrible. Gilen, I feel ill. What's happening?'

The oar slid through her fingers and Tessa flinched, taking the whole force of the water. Tears glittered on Luz's cheeks. In another second the oar would break free. Tessa peered at Gilen and saw his teeth biting on his bottom lip. His arms were shaking, trying to hold on to his own oar.

'I don't know. There's something I want to think and I can't. He must have left a thought-shield here. I know something's wrong but I don't know what.' He swallowed and managed to tighten his grip again.

'I think we're going away from it, again. Luz, think of Mother and Scouros. Pretend you aren't really here.'

It was exactly midnight and they were bone-tired. Tod thought the river was slowing down but he was too miserable to say anything. His eyes closed and he shook them open. There had not been a bridge for ten minutes. When the shock came, none of them were expecting it. The river banks had been battered by the current. Pieces had broken away. The rowing boat hit the tree trunk with a deafening crash. The next minute Tod was on his stomach on the bottom of the boat, an oar and Luz's feet under his ribs. There had been so much noise he had hardly noticed the first splash. Then he heard Gilen yell 'Tessa!' and saw him jump. Seconds later, Sheeni followed.

The boat spun broadside to the current. Tod heard the rudder snap. The other oar whipped over him and into the water. Zoo slid overboard, a branch caught in his back pack, dragging him into the river. Foaming waves swept into the boat.

'Zoo! Let it go! Let go, Zoo!!'

Zoo ripped the shoulder tabs off his jacket and the pack splashed into the dark Thames and vanished. For a moment he kicked and struggled, almost washed away by the current. Then he heaved and slumped down in the puddle of water at the bottom of the boat. His face wobbled like a chocolate blancmange.

'It's all right, Zoo. Help me get this oar into the water. See if the rudder's any use.' Tod took a breath. He suddenly felt ten feet tall and as strong as an elephant. He was not afraid. 'Luz, are you all right?'

She was nodding and sobbing at the same time. They has lost one oar, half of their rudder and Zoo's pack. Worst of all, they had split their group down the middle. Three were still in the boat. Three had been swallowed by the black night and icy water. The Wise One's words rang in their ears. They should never, never split up.

* * *

Tessa gasped and tried to think. Her clothes held her up for the first seconds and they kept her body warm. Her face was freezing wet and her hood dragged in the water, but she did not panic. She remembered what Gilen had said and slid one arm free of her pack, crawled on top of it and twiddled the chemical light until it reacted with the water. The orange glow lit her face. The water carried her along like a cork, the warm light right under her nose. She had been so surprised to fall overboard she had not even screamed. They might not have noticed. But Gilen had promised. He had promised to be with her if they had to swim.

'Tessa!' Gilen's voice, swallowing water and coughing. 'Tessa shout. I can't see you.'

'Gilen!' Her throat hurt and she had to stop herself crying with relief. 'Gilen, I'm here. I can see your light!'

'I can see yours, too. Hold on, I'm coming. Sheeni, follow.'

She saw the white shape of the dog first, splashing along with his mouth grinning and lapping at the water. He looked as if he was enjoying the game. Gilen's arm sliced through the waves next to her and his eyes glittered with fun.

'That's woken me up, anyway. Cold, isn't it? Get hold of my belt. We're heading for the shore.'

She watched him take a firm grip on Sheeni's collar as well. Instead of swimming across the current, Gilen swam with it, moving slowly towards the bank. The current actually helped them along.

72

He headed for the part of the shore that curved towards them. He was a powerful swimmer and Sheeni added four extra legs.

Before the cold had eaten through Tessa's clothes, the three swimmers slithered on frozen mud, climbing a flight of concrete steps and finally stood in London, the Old Capital of Britain. Somewhere, Tod, Luz and Zoo were either rowing to safety or being carried out to sea. But she would not cry. If Gilen could be brave, so could she. They rolled in the dry snow to soak most of the water out of their clothes and Gilen made her jump up and down until she was warm. His wet hair was standing on end and Tessa grinned at him. Then they started to look for a safe place to hide. When it was light, they would have to find the others. They just had to find them.

FROZEN LONDON

A fine rain had been falling when Tod tied an ice pick to the end of a rope and swung it over the water. On the fifth swing, he had tangled it in a fallen tree and the boat had swung sideways against the current. After half an hour of a hand-over-hand tug of war, they had managed to drag the boat out of the river. The temperature had still been falling and Zoo's fluffy eyebrows had frozen. The three friends had staggered through icy bushes to a hut in the shelter of a massive crane, piling inside and barricading the door with old furniture. Then they had slept like the dead.

'Zoo, wake up. I can't open the door.'

A boot tickled under his ribs and Zoo snorted awake. His hat had slid over his eyes. When he tugged it away, Luz was standing there, glaring down at him. She was dark blue and that meant trouble.

'I thought you were supposed to be on watch?' she said.

'I thought Tod was on watch.' The two boys had shared a blanket and a heat-pack. The warmth must have been too much for Tod's tired body. He was snoring against Zoo's shoulder. 'Why won't the door open?'

Zoo stumbled to the door and gave it a hearty

shove. There was a cracking sound but the door stayed shut. Surprised, he tried again and used more of his weight. It was like pushing a brick wall. Behind him, Tod was still half asleep, groaning and rubbing at his stiff arms. Zoo gritted his teeth, put all of his weight on his left foot and lunged at the door. The crunch of breaking glass made Tod sit up, babbling with shock. The hinges snapped and the door clattered onto the snow. Birdsong and brilliant sunshine flooded inside.

'It's ice! It had frozen shut.' Zoo blew a large, white cloud. 'Tod, come and see. Everything's frozen.'

Even with the heat-pack glowing like a barbecue, cold fingers seemed to push between the floorboards. Tod stood up and joined the others at the door.

'It's like another world,' he whispered.

London had frozen. Thick ice glittered as far as they could see. Every building could have been carved from a single diamond and every carved diamond was frosted with climbing ivy. Long grasses had turned to white needles between bushes with icy flowers on their branches. Trees had grown through the roads and climbers twined around the cranes and lamp-posts.

'It's amazing!'

Zoo shook his head and watched two cats stalk along the top of a rubbish skip filled with frozen foxgloves. Rabbits scratched the snow away to nibble at the frozen grass. Birds were everywhere, puffing their feathers out against the cold and singing at the tops of their voices.

'If Tessa and Gilen are out in this they'll be frozen stiff.' Zoo was thinking out loud and forgot whose brother and sister he was talking to. 'It must still be point two of a degree below freezing in the topsoil. No nid could burrow through it.'

Tod had seen Luz's face. 'Don't worry, they're

bound to be somewhere safe. You know what Gilen's like. He thinks of just about everything. Look at all the plants!'

Of course, there had been no one here to weed or trim. London was a frozen garden.

'They'll look for us down-river. We'll have to go up-river to meet them.' Zoo busily arranged the stove for breakfast. 'The only trouble is, the grey men will be looking for us along the river banks. We'll have to be careful they don't see us before we see them.'

A sparrow landed on the doorstep and started to scratch the back of its head with one claw. Its eyes glittered with curiosity and it let Luz walk right up to it before it fluttered away. A small group of birds gathered on the rubbish skip, one on the lookout for cats, the rest watching the three people inside the hut. They stretched their wings out in the sun and Luz smiled.

'No, you're right, Tod. I'd know if they were hurt. But I wish they were here, right now. Twins shouldn't be apart.'

After a breakfast of warm oats and honey, the threesome set off along the river bank. Last night they had lost a fifth of their food stock. Better not to think of that.

They were in the heart of the old docklands. Icy meadow grass scrunched under their boots leaving the only human footprints they could see. They passed huddles of old sheds, towering warehouses and sudden inlets that had once held ships. It would have been lonely, but animal tracks and piles of rabbit-droppings covered the snow. Cats lazed in every dry patch of sun or rubbed against Zoo's boots and purred. The rabbits were so tame that Tod could stroke between the babies' ears and the sky seemed to be full of birds. At least they weren't alone.

Luz pulled a map from her back pack. 'According to this we're miles away from the City. And we're probably miles away from Gilen and Tessa, as well. If we're going to see them, we ought to be high up, looking down.'

Zoo and Luz both looked at Tod and he felt himself blush. 'It they're miles away, we still wouldn't see them,' he said.

'We would if we were up there with your binoculars.'

He should have guessed. Luz had already decided what they should do. Tod turned around and saw the building on the opposite side of the river. He had read about it in school. On the day the King had declared it open, the electricity in London had finally died. The King had been cutting through the tape when all the video cameras and microphones had stopped working. That had been eleven in the morning, Thursday 30th July 2582, two hundred years ago.

'The Rotherhithe Tower,' Luz said. 'We should be able to see right into the City from up there. If you're too frightened, Zoo and I'll just borrow your binoculars.'

'Don't be stupid!' Tod glared at her. 'It's a snerd-brained idea. Anyone could look up and see us looking down.'

Zoo looked embarrassed. 'Stop it, you two. We shouldn't argue and you know we couldn't leave Tod behind, Luz. We've got to stay together.'

'Well.' Tod gritted his teeth. 'Well, I'm not going up there, and that's final!'

'"And that's final!"' Luz imitated his voice and sneered at him. 'You're the snerd-brain, Tod Barrett. And you're a scaredy-scaredy!'

'All right! We'll go up your globby tower!' Tod's voice quivered with anger. 'Just don't blame me when we get up there and find ourselves surrounded by grey men. And what happens if they see us when we're in the middle of the river? There's nowhere to hide in all of that ice.'

Nowhere to swim either. Frustrated ducks waddled up and down, pecking at the glittery waves and quacking angrily. A pair of swans glided out of the sky, ready to land in a river, and found themselves skating along on their tail feathers.

Zoo tested the ice. If it would hold his weight, it was bound to hold Tod and Luz. He tried one foot, then both, then bounced out from the bank. Three bounces and the ice held. He nodded. 'I think it's safe.'

Tod stamped off the snowy bank, put one foot on the ice and slid sideways, waving his arms about for balance. Seconds later, they were all flat on their backs in a crowd of ducks.

'The snow's caked solid on our boots. I can't break it off, it's like concrete!' Zoo attacked the layer of white sticking to his soles. It refused to budge. 'We need skates.' He decided. 'That's the one thing missing in the back packs. Let's hold hands and keep each other up.'

They set off over the frozen ripples and cracks of ice. The sky was brilliant white without a hint of blue, and the air was so full of light it made the edges of the ice-buildings sparkle and crackle.

Up ahead, the Rotherhithe Tower grew into a giant gull colony. Its windows were broken and gulls flew in and out of the shattered panes. Other birds perched on the ivy-covered walls and the noise of squawking and whistling made Tod wince. When he winced, he forgot he was walking on ice. The snowy soles of his boots skidded and he pulled Luz after him.

By the time they reached the tower, they were

covered in bruises. They stopped just outside the main doors and Tod shivered. 'I think we should turn our jackets inside out. There might be grey men.'

Tod and Zoo reversed their white jackets and were suddenly bright orange. Luz's silver feathers sparkled like white fire.

Zoo frowned. 'I hope there's no creepies in there. I hate creepies. I wish I'd got a torch.'

Ice had coated the inside of the Tower as well. Every inch of floor, wall and ceiling was thick with grey ice. The staircase was a solid, spiral slide up to the roof. Frozen creepers covered the lower windows and the light was cold and green like sea water.

'Well, it looks like being a hard climb.' Zoo glanced at Tod's pale face. 'Don't worry, we'll help each other. It can't be all that difficult.'

He was wrong. The climb up the frozen stairs was exhausting. They roped themselves together and Zoo led the way upwards, a step at a time. At each step, he hacked the ice pick into the frozen stair-rail and held on until the others reached him. When he was dripping with the effort, Tod took over. Seagulls flew around their heads, squealing.

'You know something? If this ice stays, everything's going to starve.' Tod clung to the ice pick and tried to get his breath back. 'The nids can't come above ground, so they can't eat. The ice on the river will stop the gulls feeding. Things will start dying.'

Zoo nodded. His brown face was sad. 'Two or three days of ice, maximum. I hope our supplies last out. All of this exercise is making me hungry. I'm on only one stomach already.' His empty stomach gurgled and he patted it. 'It's as hollow as a bucket-ball.'

They rested on each new floor and hugged themselves to keep warm. As long as they moved, their blood circulated quickly and they hardly felt the cold. When they sat on the ice, even the Scouran snow-clothes couldn't keep the chill out.

The door to the roof was wide open and, after two hours of struggling up the stairs, they finally staggered outside. Tod made a gulping noise and sat down, both hands over his eyes.

They were surrounded by sky and bright air. No roof, no walls. The seagulls wanted to know what they were up to. One landed on Tod's hat and stood on its red legs, pecking at the stitches. Tod yelled and the bird flew off again.

'Tod! Don't be silly.' Luz prodded him with her foot. 'You're all right, anyway. You know you can fly.'

'I don't!' Tod's voice was muffled by his arms. 'That's what he said and I think he's wrong. I can't fly. I can't even look!'

He managed to open one eye and squint at the sky between his fingers. Zoo looked sympathetic but Luz stamped about impatiently. She still thought he was stupid to be afraid of high places. She could go right to the edge of the building and look down at the tiny, tiny trees and not feel anything. Only babies were frightened of heights. When she had been younger, she had crawled all over the castle walls and never once felt scared of falling.

'Come on, Tod. We have to look for the others. It's too cold to stand around. You know we wouldn't let you fall over.'

Luz started to jump up and down to warm her toes. The gulls flew around her and she tried to catch one and missed. Gilen would have caught it without trying.

Luz was suddenly very sad and she let her mind wander back to Scouros; their mother and father laughing; Gilen always torn between joining in and staying serious; and her own giggles ringing through the Great Hall. She realized how much she was missing her twin. Twins were supposed to stay together until they were adult-old. Her heart thudded and she felt her eyes sting. One minute she was bouncing along, the next she had slid over the edge.

Zoo gasped. 'Tod! She's fallen over!'

Tod leapt to his feet and fell over and leapt up again. The whole building seemed to spin around him. Luz's squeals were already getting fainter. Before he could stop himself, he had jumped after her.

Tod screamed. He was falling downwards and the hard ice roared up at him. Something flapped next to his knee. A bird had followed him down and it watched him with beady black eyes. Tod wanted to grab it and ride back up to the roof on its wings.

Where was Luz? Tod gritted his teeth, rolled and shot sideways, just missing the wall. The bird flapped away, squealing. Tod slid the other way, both arms groping at the air. He started to spin around very slowly.

Luz saw the ground closing in on her. She was cold all over and she wanted to cry. It was unfair. Every time she showed off, something bad happened.

'Wheee!! Luz, Luz, look! Yahoooooeeeeeyy!'

A boy in an orange jacket flashed past her, a silly grin on his face. It was Tod.

'Tod! Stop playing!' She could see the tops of the trees. 'Tod!! Stop it! Help me, nid-mouth!'

He grabbed her by the hood and she found herself hanging with her arms somewhere above her head. Tod was still whooping and swinging her around and she wanted to thump him but her hands could not reach. Then she surprised herself by bursting into tears.

81

'It's all right, Luz. I won't let you fall. This is AMAZING!!'

Luz sniffed and glared up at him. 'Amazing for you. I don't like it.' And her face curled up and she cried again.

Zoo watched the two of them come back over the edge of the roof. His knees buckled and he sat on the ice. That was it, then. The old man had been right. All they had to do was fight their fears and they would have their secret powers to help them. But they had to find Tessa and Gilen . . . If Tessa and Gilen were still alive.

Tod lowered Luz onto the roof and she pushed him away. 'I'm all right! Stop fussing. I'm just . . .' She had to sniff. 'I'm just missing Gilen. I'm not as strong when he isn't around. I'm cold.'

Luz was clutching a heat-pack, covered in seagulls, with the two boys patting her on the shoulders, when the sky turned black. The birds stopped squealing and everyone stared upwards. Just one second. A black sky and then the smell of cabbage and the cold, cold wind blowing the birds away. Zoo knocked Tod down and they grabbed Luz, lying flat on the ice with the wind dragging at the legs of their trousers. The wind passed over them and the sun started to warm their backs. They all sat up and stared at each other.

'The Betrayer's here.' Luz closed her eyes. 'He's here and we're still separated. And I can't feel Gilen anywhere . . .'

WIKKIT AND THE PIG-MEN

Tessa woke up to find Sheeni curled next to her, a heavy paw on her knee. His eyes pleaded for her to stroke him in his favourite spot, between his red ears. Gilen had stayed awake all night and he looked thinner and very pale. When he knew she was awake, he smiled and Sheeni's tail banged on the floor.

'He wants his breakfast. I'm afraid it'll have to be cold.'

Tessa remembered that Luz had the stove.

They were in a small room lined with video screens. Gilen thought it was a security station looking over the warehouse. Now it was very empty. Every table was bare, every filing cabinet locked. Tessa took the Firebird feather out of her vest and stroked it while Gilen spread his maps.

'We must be somewhere past Tower Bridge. We went under it in the water. I could see the shape of the towers.' He ran his finger over the blue line of the river. 'The question is, do we go up-river and hope the others catch up with us or do we go down-river and try to find them?'

'I think we should try to find them first. Gilen, what if they went right out to sea?'

His finger stopped moving and he looked up at

her. 'If they've gone, I'll make sure you're safe, then I'll fight the Betrayer on my own.'

The room turned cold. It wasn't the cold of the snow, it was the cold of evil. Sheeni's white hair rose and he backed away, growling. Gilen's eyes widened and the blue gold glittered above them. Blue sparks crackled down his arms and his fingernails curled like a cat's. Then the cold had gone and he was just a boy again. Sometimes Tessa was afraid of him.

'Was that the Betrayer?' Tessa whispered.

He nodded. 'He's come looking for me. Hurry and eat. I don't want to stay in one place too long.'

The heat-pack had kept the walls free of ice and Tessa had seen the small hole in the floorboards without really thinking about it. When a tiny head popped out, she squawked and nearly fell over Sheeni. Two bright eyes and a nose full of whiskers . . .

Gilen smiled. 'Hello, Wikkit. We're friends. Come and talk.'

The brown mouse called Wikkit scuttled into the room and onto Gilen's outstretched hand.

'I wonder . . .' Gilen stroked the mouse's fur and it sat up on his palm and washed itself. 'I wonder if this little thing knows what's going on.'

Tessa was still recovering from her jump of shock. She had expected Yellow Eyes to appear, not a furry animal. 'How could it know?' Then, frowning, 'And how would you ask it? Can you speak to mice as well?'

Gilen grinned at her and gave the mouse a biscuit crumb. 'I can speak to anything that has a brain in it . . . Even Luz.'

Tessa had to smile back. She settled down with an arm around Sheeni and watched Gilen's eyes close. He was thinking words into the mouse's head and she saw Wikkit become completely still. The fur rose on the back of his neck and he started to squeak and wave his front paws around. He sounded angry.

The conversation did not last long. Gilen broke a biscuit onto the floor and the mouse shot back into his hole. Seconds later, he had brought his whole family, from grandparents to tiny babies, and they fell on the crumbs like tiny vultures. The babies were so beautiful! Tessa longed to cuddle them. Sheeni growled and she held his neck.

'Sheeni, no.' Gilen frowned. 'That was very interesting. Wikkit says there's an evil place no animal goes, somewhere in the Centre. They call it the "Bad Tree". What does it make you think of? Remember that history lesson.'

'The Grey Needle!' Tessa stared at him. 'You read it and you wouldn't say what the words meant . . .'

'And I still won't. They're dangerous words.'

Gilen stood up and tidied his back pack, adjusting the straps until they were more comfortable. He ignored Tessa's angry face and in the end she just sighed and strapped her own pack in place. It was no good sulking. If Gilen wanted to keep a secret, nothing would budge him.

Wikkit had eaten enough. He scurried to Gilen's feet and started to speak again. Gilen looked interested. 'I think we're doing a deal. He says there are very young babies in the nests and another lot on the way. They'll die in this cold.'

Wikkit twitched his ears towards the heat-pack.

'Ah!' Gilen nodded. 'He wants us to leave the heat-pack. It will save his nest . . . And he wants to come with us.'

The mouse mimed a snarling, squeaking fight, sending Sheeni whimpering for cover.

'He says he'll look after us!'

Tessa met Gilen eyes. She could see that he liked

the idea of being protected by a mouse. When she pulled a face, he grinned at her.

'Never underestimate small animals. I have a feeling we'll need all the help we can get.' Gilen knelt on the floor. 'Wikkit, you've got a deal. I'll see you don't go hungry.'

Wikkit scampered back to his family to give them the news.

Gilen stopped grinning. 'Before we go, I'm going to try to "see" Luz.' He looked down and clenched his toes in his boots. 'I don't think it'll be easy.'

He pressed both fists against his forehead and concentrated. Tessa saw his eyes pale to silver-white and sweat trickle under his fingers. Before she knew what she was doing, she had put her arm around his shoulders.

It was like being inside a church belfry when all of the bells rang. The thoughts flew out of Gilen's head, thousands and thousands of words crashing into Tessa's brain. She heard the Scouran and the Capital-speak and the strange, musical magic of Gilen's Old Language.

'Little Sister, hear me. I can't see you. I can't hear you. Where are you, Luz? How far away. How far . . . far . . .? Let me see you, Luz. We need each other now.'

Tessa staggered backwards and felt Gilen grab her arm. His eyes blinded her and she shivered. Then he was just Gilen again, biting his lip and too thin.

'I frightened you, Tessa. I'm sorry.'

'It's OK. I shouldn't have touched you when you were thinking hard.' She swallowed and pretended to be smiling at the mice. 'You didn't find her, did you?'

'No, I couldn't even guess which direction she's moving in. In fact, I couldn't feel her mind at all.' He pulled his gloves on very carefully. 'There's something blocking me, Tessa. It was like shouting into the wind. She can't have heard me.'

He turned away and held his hand out for Wikkit. The mouse clawed his way up the white sleeve and into the top of Gilen's collar, sitting on the little hollow over his collarbone. His nose pointed out, bristling whiskered excitement, and he squeaked farewell to his family nest.

* * *

Last night they had staggered out of the river, almost too cold to talk, and Tessa had followed blindly. Now she realized how far they had walked inland. There was no sign of the Thames, just towering ice-blocks of warehouses, frozen grass and trees full of pigeons. The pigeons came to land on Gilen's shoulder and he talked to them and fed them. If he kept that up, there would be no food left for himself.

'They're going to fly overhead and keep watch for us. That's worth a few crumbs on a cold morning, Tessa.'

Sometimes she wished he couldn't read her mind so easily. She caught him grinning at her and grinned back, blushing.

They walked quickly, taking it in turns to go first, one watching the other's back and Sheeni sniffing everywhere and forgetting to look like a guard-dog. Every so often, red ears would twitch, white tail would wag and Sheeni would charge head first into a frozen bush to send a cat spitting away.

The warehouses crowded closer together. The last pigeon was out of sight and the air was damp. No sun touched the ground between the overhanging pipes and ivy. Gilen had wanted to go up-river. He was probably right. How could they hope to see the others when this mass of buildings towered over their heads? Some of the narrow alleys were bridged with rusty iron and the ground underneath was completely dark. Unless the pigeons could be trusted to look out for Tod as well as the grey men . . . ? When Gilen put his hand on Tessa's shoulder she squawked with fright.

'Sorry . . .' He grinned at her, then became completely serious. 'I think we should move out of here. The Hargs like dark places.'

They had walked into an older area. The warehouses were red under the ice, hidden bricks instead of hidden concrete. Wooden planks stuck out of the snow to one side of the alleyway and Tessa's feet felt unsafe. Cellars down there, she thought. Gilen was right, this was a bad place to be.

Sheeni sniffed just out of sight and Tessa smiled. The dog was still a puppy. He should have been guarding his master. Sniff, sniff. He must have found something interesting, he sounded like a blocked vacuum-cleaner. Wikkit suddenly squeaked and dived inside Gilen's shirt. A pigeon swooped down, screaming warning.

Gilen gasped. 'That isn't Sheeni!'

Then he pushed her out of the way and a door in the warehouse wall crashed open.

Tessa slid on the sloping ice. Then she saw the fat man with the face like a pig and screamed and fell. The ground broke under her feet and she was half-way into a gaping hole. She grabbed at a plank and twisted away, frantically. She was going to fall down into the dark cellar. If she did, she'd just die. Tessa threw her legs sideways and felt the back pack fall. The next minute she was free.

Three men. The sniffer-man with the pig-nose and two of the grey, tall, iron-hard men they had met at the river. Gilen's whole body tensed, waiting for their first move, and it was Tessa who saw the white shape come wagging around the corner.

'Sheeni, hunt!' she yelled.

The sniffer-man turned towards Sheeni, the others grabbed for Gilen, but he ducked under their arms. He twisted on one foot and kicked out with the other. One grey head banged against the wall.

Sheeni hit the sniffer-man in the middle of his fat belly and bit for his neck, but the man was strong. His body wormed inside his clothes like a snake in its skin. Suddenly, Sheeni was yelping with fright as the pig-face split open.

Gilen turned and saw the sniffer-man's mouth opening, as wide as a library book. Horrible. It was studded with teeth as long and stained as tent pegs.

'Sheeni! Roll!'

Gilen ran to help Sheeni and did not see the grey man's hand or the slimy, grey blade, but the smell was strong enough to turn a mouse's stomach. Wikkit dug ten front claws into Gilen's neck, just in time. The knife missed the boy's arm by a hair's width. It hit the brick wall behind him and its blade cracked along one edge. There was a puff of green steam and a thin trickle of poison slid free.

Gilen saw the mist of poison-drops float towards him. One hand automatically pushed Wikkit's nose into the safety of his jacket. He was diving for the ground when he realized that the poison was in his lungs. His mouth opened and he heard himself gurgle and cough. Funny. It didn't hurt. The cold, metal taste spread from his tongue and into his blood. Into his heart. He shivered. The pig-man might hurt Tessa . . . Or Sheeni and Wikkit. Tod would never forgive him. He had promised to protect Tessa. Then he wondered what it would be like to die. His body was cold before it hit the ice.

Tessa screamed and threw herself onto the pig-man's back. She bit into his ear as hard as she could. Underneath his arms, Sheeni howled with pain. The pig-man swung his elbow back to hit her but she bit deeper and he threw Sheeni aside, using both hands to reach behind him. His fingers dug into Tessa's arms and ripped her free, like a bull flicking a fly away with its tail. She skidded over the ice into the pile of planks.

The three men closed in on Gilen's curled-up body. They were laughing at the small shape swearing mouse-curses. What could a mouse do? A grey man lifted his fist to knock the tiny pest away. There was death in his smile. And Wikkit gave a high squeal. Higher and higher . . . Out of a human ear's hearing. It drove the three men back, clutching their ears in agony.

Gilen's back pack was against the wall where the men had thrown it. Tessa's hands shook but she tugged the buckles open, making herself stay calm. She pulled out the blanket and the maps and the roll of rope. Her fingers closed around a bundle of cigar-shaped tubes and the strange, wide-nozzled pistol. She pushed a flare into the barrel, aimed at the sky between the warehouse walls and fired.

The bang made the three men turn. They took a step towards her, threateningly. The next minute, the whole sky was blood-red. It hurt her own eyes, but the grey men shrieked and covered their faces, staggering into the wall. Tessa fired another flare and yellow flames blossomed in the air. The whole world was sun-bright and yellow. Pig-face opened his mouth in a roar of pain. The bristles around his snout writhed and twisted. It was too much. The men stumbled, bouncing from wall to wall as they fled from the light.

Sheeni cried and pawed at Gilen's arm, not under-standing why his young master did not move. Wikkit stood on his back legs, front claws patting up and down Gilen's chin, trying to find some movement.

90

Blue blood trickled down Gilen's neck and into the snow. Tessa knew that he was badly hurt.

The medicines were in her pack and the pack was in the cellar. Quite suddenly, there was no point at all in being afraid of the dark and of small places. If she stood here she would watch her friend die. His head was cut open at the back and his skin had turned a strange, silvery blue. She knew that he was injured and she guessed that he was poisoned as well. There were greenish flecks, like the spray from a fizzy drink, all over his mouth. It must have been a poisoned knife.

Tessa tied a rope to the strongest of the wooden planks, gripped the chemical torch between her teeth, then slid through the hole and down into the darkness.

The ice had set in weird shapes and black shadows chased each other and put thin claws out to touch her legs. Old crates had been gnawed away by rats. The nids would not let rats come into their territory and so the rats had to fend for themselves outside New Capital. Some country people claimed to have seen rats five feet long.

Tessa's fingers slipped on the rope and she landed very hard. She could not see the pack anywhere. Maybe the rats had eaten it. When a face appeared at the top of the hole she yelped, then realized it was only Sheeni. With the dog whining down at her, she made herself stand and walk between the crates. There were two dead rats in a pile of snow in the corner. And the back pack, half-hidden by scattered papers. She grabbed it, fumbled it over her arms, then ran to the rope. She was so frightened, she shinned up it like a monkey.

Her hands felt strange. All the warmth in the world had run into her fingers and they were tingling. Tessa sat next to Gilen and put one hand on

his hair, the other against the crooked scar. The
tingling spread up her arms and down her spine
and settled in the pit of her stomach. She knew what
it was. Her power. She tried not to be afraid and let
the warmth spread out of her and into the terrible,
choking cold inside Gilen's body. She could see
the poison inside him and its green mists were
everywhere. He would have died before she could
have found a medicine to cure him.

Gilen's mouth twisted and he started to cough.
No one should cough like that. It lifted his back right
off the ground. The poison hung on and the coughs
ripped it free. The blood suddenly ran over the
snow, bright, bright blue. Tessa heard herself tell it
to stop. It did. She told the poison to go away. For
a moment, nothing seemed to happen. Gilen had
stopped coughing. Slowly, the silver faded out of
his skin and left him just his usual blue-pink. Tessa
saw him swallow and shiver. His eyes opened and
he sat bolt upright, staring at her.

'You've found your power, Tessa,' he said.

'I went into the cellar. I'll just look after Sheeni.'

For some reason she felt shy again. Sheeni jumped
up and down, barking and crying at the same time.
He was wild with happiness to see his master alive
and never noticed Tessa touch his side, only that the
pain went away. He leapt onto his hind legs and
started to lick his master's face until a pair of hands
pushed him away and the master was laughing. A
licking dog in one hand, a whiskery mouse in the
other . . .

'Stop it! Stupid animals.' Gilen stood up and
watched Tessa put the flares back into the pack.
'Thank you.'

It was almost evening. After lighting the whole
sky with the flares, they had to get out of that area
as fast as possible. Tessa did not complain when

they did not stop for lunch or admit that she knew where they were going. They had changed direction. They were not looking for the others any more.

The sun slowly reddened and disappeared into the City. The air was colder and Tessa ached from head to foot. She was too tired to notice Gilen slow to a crawl.

'Tessa, we'd better rest for the night. I think we're safe for a while.'

Tessa squinted into the darkness and saw the entrance to an old shop. The door was open and she could just make out rows of shelves.

Gilen smiled. 'There's food as well. Look, tins everywhere.'

The shelves were piled high with frozen cans. Gilen pulled one down and rubbed the frost away with his sleeve, then he started to laugh. 'I don't believe it! Baked beans! It's a pity Vinny isn't here, he'd feel right at home.'

They raided the back of the shop for pots and pans. Then Gilen lit a fire in an old pressure cooker and held a smaller pan of frozen beans over the flames. The sweet smell of melting tomato sauce filled the air and Sheeni started to drool and roll his eyes for food. Tessa had to admit that baked beans never tasted so good.

The shop was very dark and very quiet. Tessa curled up in her sleeping bag, holding the heat-pack against her ribs, and listened to Sheeni snore. When she said Gilen's name he pretended to be asleep, but she knew that he was awake, waiting for the grey men to come again.

FIREBIRD FLIGHT

'My feet hurt.' Luz stopped walking. 'My back hurts and my arms hurt and my head hurts. It's all right for him.'

Tod was somewhere overhead, peering through his binoculars. Every now and then, he crossed the sun in a trail of seagulls.

Zoo nibbled his last frosted peardrop and chased a hungry sparrow from his shoulder. 'It's the only way we're going to find the others, Luz.' He offered her a bite of peardrop. 'Anyway, it proves that the Wise One was right. I'm trying to think what I'm frightened of so I can get my power . . . Hey, what's that?'

A grinding, slithering noise and it was coming their way! They threw themselves into a snow drift behind a frozen hedge.

The sail appeared first, a huge black square ballooning out with the wind; then the boat-shaped sled with the flashing runners and the faces, grey as stone, peering out over the sides.

Luz craned forwards. 'Now that's exactly what we need! I'll stop them.'

Zoo tried to yell 'No!'. The crack of breaking ice stopped him. Every grey face turned towards them . . . And other faces. Faces with the snouts and bristles of giant pigs.

'Oh snurks, I don't like the look of them! Luz, you've given us away.'

'I know.' She smiled smugly. 'They'll come over here and we'll go over there. Simple.'

'Except that they won't leave the boat unguarded,' Zoo groaned. 'You'll get us both caught.'

Luz started to slither backwards. 'No I won't. Look, they're coming. We can run over the ice and I'll break it behind us so they can't get back.'

'It's a trap.' Zoo stuffed two frids into his cheek pouches for comfort. 'It's a trap, I know it's a trap. They can't be that stupid.'

Luz snorted. 'Of course they can. You worry too much.'

There was nothing for it. Zoo lay belly-flat and squirmed after her. On the ice, a figure with patched trousers and a felt hat searched for them. It was the Dream-Seller. The man called out across the river and Zoo gulped. He hated that voice. It was like . . . like . . . like treacle syrup pouring over a bun.

'Here, little ones! Come to me, little children. What are you afraid of, Prince of Scouros? Are you all cowards?'

Luz laughed with relief. 'They haven't caught Gilen! Did you hear? They think he's with us. Come on!'

Her feet kicked and she slid onto the river bank. A skid and a jump and she was sprinting over the ice, boots scrunching towards the wind-sled. Zoo thundered after her, his feet sending angry ducks quacking into the air and both stomachs gurgling with fright. He thought the Dream-Seller laughed.

Half-way to the boat and Luz's face lost its blue. 'Zoo, I can't break the ice behind us!'

Zoo heard a quiet little sparking noise. The next moment, a huge sheet of grey flame sprang out of the ice. It blocked their path with a wall of fire. Luz skidded to a halt.

'Come on, Luz,' Zoo panted. 'Look, it isn't real fire, the ice isn't melting. It's just to scare us.'

He tried to catch her hand but she pulled it away, shuddering. Then he knew that Luz was afraid of fire.

'Luz, remember Tod. This is your test.' Behind him, the laughing voices were louder. 'We'll jump right through it. The ice isn't even wet. If that fire was only slightly warm, the ice would be melting.'

'I can't.' She shivered. 'I can't, Zoo. The Betrayer killed our family with fire. He burnt the castle. It was horrible.'

That was why they were using fire now. Clever.

'Even the stones burnt, Zoo. Brother Gyus took us out through the cellars or we would all have died.' Luz sniffed and swallowed. 'I'm so frightened, I can't move my feet.'

'If Tod can fly, you can run through cold fire. You have to, Luz, or we're both dead. I won't leave you.'

It was the only thing Zoo could think of. If Luz stayed here, he would be caught with her.

Luz's face quivered and she suddenly screamed at the top of her voice and threw herself at the wall of flames. The moment she touched it, it vanished. The sled was only steps away.

Luz jumped over the side of the boat, straight into the waiting arms of a pig-faced man. Another opened his whole face in a grunt of welcome. 'Zoo, it's a trap! Run!'

Zoo had no intention of running. He was a Trimonese. He nodded, politely. 'I'm sure we can talk about this. Your master must have told you not to hurt us? I mean, I suppose he wants to work something out?'

The pig-man laughed. 'He want you dead. I kill you, little mushroom!'

Gilen had been right. They could not listen to plain, good sense. Zoo launched himself and crushed the second pig-face into the bottom of the boat. Grunts of anger kept him still for a moment, and Zoo kicked the other one in the ribs. It loosened the man's grip and Luz twisted free. A pig-hand snapped shut on her pack and ripped it open. Plates and spoons and pans clattered into the boat.

Luz scrambled to her knees. 'Zoo, the others are coming!'

'Break the ice!' He gritted his teeth. 'I'll handle these two.'

The sound of breaking ice seemed to give the pig-men extra strength. Zoo hit the wooden rail, pongy pig-breath freezing his face. He tried to yell to Luz to run and saw her grab the frying-pan and bounce it off the two men's heads. Three bonks of metal on bristly skulls. She might have been using a feather.

A white shape fell from nowhere. Two hands closed over one piggy ear and a pig-man squealed in pain. Mouth open, Zoo watched the man shoot up from the boat, then down, very fast. A loud splash and he was choking in the icy water.

Tod grabbed another dirty ear. A heave and the second pig-man hit the Thames.

Yells and curses ringing in his ears, Tod came down to land. He helped Zoo pull the big brake-lever free and the metal spikes levered back into the hull of the sled. The black sail crackled outwards, filled with wind and they were off, steel runners skimming over the ice faster than a pack of nids.

Zoo rubbed his neck. 'That was good timing. Three point six seconds more and they would have throttled me.'

Luz nodded. 'And I've got my power and the

Dream-Seller hasn't found Tessa and Gilen. I'm sure we'll find them now. Then everything'll be all right. You'll see.'

* * *

As soon as the sun appeared over the window-ledge, Wikkit stretched himself awake. His blue friend had r.ot slept and he looked tired. Wikkit clambered up the white sleeve and tickled the boy's chin with his nose hairs until he laughed. They washed together, the boy from a bowl of water, Wikkit with his tiny claws sorting through his whiskers and knocking the dust out of his fur.

'Tessa it's time to go. The sun's chased the shadows away.'

Tessa smiled before she opened her eyes. When she looked up, Wikkit's tail was vanishing into Gilen's jacket.

'I'm going outside to talk to the pigeons. You'd better have breakfast . . .' Gilen grinned at her. 'Sheeni's had some food, so don't believe his big eyes . . . Greedy dog.'

Tessa washed her face in snow-water, then searched the dusty shelves for food. Anyone with a tin-opener could have made themselves a feast, but she settled for tinned pears and some of her biscuits. Sheeni rolled his eyes and moaned until she gave him a biscuit. Stroking his red ears, Tessa decided that she wanted a dog of her own. If she ever got back home. Tod and the others were probably looking for her right now. She sighed and walked out into the sunshine.

Gilen was waiting for her. 'The grey men are coming, Tessa. They aren't too close yet, but we have to leave. I think we should go back to the river.'

'Did the pigeons see Tod and the others?'

98

'No.' Gilen looked down. 'No, not yet. They're still looking. Come on, let's go.'

* * *

The sun was high and bright, sparkling on the icy buildings and snow. Tessa and Gilen had walked for hours, following the frozen Thames up-river. If Gilen was right, they would soon be in the City. From there it was a few bends in the Thames to the Houses of Parliament and the Grey Needle.

Overhead, most of London's pigeons were on the lookout for three other children. They were not looking for a massive sled sailing up the middle of the river. Wikkit suddenly appeared on top of Gilen's collar. The mouse had caught the family scent.

'Tessa, Wikkit thinks Luz is somewhere around here. I'm not sure. There's something, but it feels different. Listen . . .' His eyes narrowed. 'Can you hear a sort of grinding noise?'

Grinding, slithering . . . The noise approached at incredible speed. Gilen grabbed Tessa's hand. 'Lets head for cover.'

The big sled had been full of pig-men and waves of pig-stink came to Gilen's nose. He was too tired to take any risks. He sensed pig and grey cold and Luz . . . But not Luz. Something else was there and Wikkit nibbled Gilen's ear with excitement. Gilen's eyes widened and he burst out laughing. Sugared frid!

A shadow drifted over the ice. If it was a bird, it was the fattest thing in the skies. Gilen had already jumped onto the ice, running towards the black sled. Tessa squinted upwards. A boy flew overhead, binoculars in one hand, a large pigeon trying to settle on the other. He was a small boy, brown-haired, sharp-chinned. She could almost see the freckles.

Tessa's knees weakened with relief. 'It's Tod!' Her voice cracked and she had to swallow. 'Tod!'

Tod swerved, peered down and saw them. Then the sled skimmed towards them and Luz waved over the wooden side. Zoo's chocolate face split into a massive grin behind her. Sheeni yowled and wagged his tail and both back legs in a blur of delight. Tod swooped down from the sky and the five friends were reunited.

Tod lifted his sister by the shoulders and swung her around. 'Tess! We thought you'd drowned or frozen solid.' The sun had turned his freckles black. He looked fit and healthy, full of life. 'You won't believe it! Luz and I have both got our powers!'

Tessa laughed. 'Yes I will, 'cos I have as well! Have you seen the men with pig-noses?'

'We've fought them off!' Tod sounded proud of himself. 'We stole this sled from them. Isn't it great?'

They both stopped talking. Tessa's throat hurt and she gave Tod a hug and watched him blush but look pleased underneath.

Luz looked at her own brother. A mouse balanced on the inside of his collar. When she looked at it down her nose, it pulled a rude face at her. The little . . . ! Trust Gilen to have found help, even in the mouse-world. Trust him to have found a rude mouse! She wondered if he had missed her as much as she had missed him. He was watching Tod and Tessa.

'I got my powers by jumping off a building and Luz ran through cold fire.' Tod laughed, happily. 'Only Zoo's got to find his strength and he's bound to before long. Then we can do anything.'

Tessa glared at him and lowered her voice. 'Gilen's still the same. I don't think he's afraid of anything, not even the pig-men.' She was about to tell him about the fight and the flares when she saw Gilen's eyes watching her. 'Gilen, isn't the sled wonderful . . . ?'

Wikkit reared up on his back legs and gave an ear-splitting squeak. Tessa twisted around and Tod's fingers dug into her arm. The whole river bank erupted with animal noise. Sparrows and starlings exploded out of the hedges and the rabbits stamped warning.

'Too late. The Spirits help us.'

The blue ran out of Gilen's skin and left it a watered-down grey. His eyes had that silver glow which meant trouble. One by one, the others followed his gaze. From behind every warehouse, every bush, every ice-coated tree, the grey men walked. And the pig-men. And, smiling, the Dream-Seller, a poisoned dagger shining between his fingers. The five fugitives twisted left and right. The circle had already closed. They were surrounded.

Luz broke the ice between the circle and the sled but the men were prepared. They threw ladders and ropes over the gap and made bridges. Luz broke the bridges and the effort brought her out in a cold sweat. She had not noticed how weak her powers were. The men built more bridges and she could not break them any more.

Gilen shook his head. 'You'd only slow them down. Save your strength, Luz.' He turned away from her. 'Tod, can you carry both girls at once?'

Tod put one arm around Tessa, one around Luz and bent his knees. When he pushed up, he rose as far as his toes and sagged down, shaking. He had fought the pig-men and he had been flying ever since. He shook his head, horrified. 'I can't!'

Gilen took a deep breath. 'Take Tessa,' he said.

'No!' Tessa backed away. 'No, I'm staying with you! We have to be together! Remember what Brother Gyus said!'

Gilen smiled and Tessa turned cold from head to toe. She did not like that smile.

'Brother Gyus thought we'd all have powers but we haven't. Tessa, I'm the one they really want.' He hesitated. 'But there might be one way out, if I still can.'

Tod was bewildered. What else could Gilen do?

Luz had guessed. 'No, Gilen, you'll hurt yourself. We have to fight them together like the Wise One said.'

'Luz, I can't! I haven't found any power except the one I already had. If I don't use that, I might as well just give up and hope they let the rest of you go.' He bit his lip. 'I'm sorry. I thought I could protect you.'

Gilen knelt down, spreading his fingers on the ice.

Tessa shook Luz's arm, frantically. 'Luz, what's he doing? Why will it hurt him?'

'He's calling the Firebirds.' Luz rubbed her eyes. 'It's one of the Great Legends. Every time we've had a disaster, a High King has tried to call them but it only works for the True Leaders. It could take all of his strength. He could die, Tessa.'

The grey men were closer. Pig-snorts and cold, cold laughter. The whiff of poison sickly on the air . . .

Gilen said the Old Words and tried to stop thinking about the Dream-Seller and the pig-men. It was easy enough to pull one feather out of the air . . . Trying to bring a whole bird was something else. His head started to hurt very badly. Wikkit slid into the top of his collar to give him some furry warmth, but the ice was in his bones.

Zoo heard them first, a distant whoosh and flap of giant wings. He gulped and stared upwards. 'They're flying out of the sun! Tod, Tessa . . . Look at that!'

A single, silvery cloud had slid over the sun. As Zoo pointed, the cloud split open and golden fire blazed across the sky. Giant wings threw the light onto the snow and every grey man howled with terror and pain.

Tessa gasped. 'They're beautiful!'

'They're dangerous.' Luz shuddered. 'I didn't think they really existed. No one's tried to call them for hundreds of years.'

The three birds skimmed through the air and their long claws shone silver-sharp. The white light of the sun's heart was in their eyes and Tod knew where he had seen it before. Gilen's eyes had burned like that when he had thrown Vinny Morgan into the biology pond.

The ice melted as the birds landed. The hot air from their wings blew the girls' plaits backwards and the icy ground shook under their claws. Each bird was taller than a horse and they glared around them, scornfully. They were from the Old Scouran World, like Gilen's throw-dart. If he said the wrong words they might claw him to death.

The biggest bird opened her beak and crackled a laugh. 'Who are you, blue boy? What do you want? Quickly or we'll come so close your nose will burn.'

Gilen stood up. A circle of grey men cowered on the ice, hands over faces. He felt Wikkit squeeze back inside his shirt, small claws a-scrabble.

'I'm Gilen Erath, the last High Prince of Scouros. My friends and I need your help or the grey men will kill us in front of you.'

The bird stalked forwards and Gilen breathed the golden flames. The heat stung his eyes and he blinked, hoping the birds didn't think he was crying with fear.

The bird's harsh voice clacked and rattled in her

beak. 'So, you know the Old Words, little Prince? What else do you know?'

'This.'

Gilen lifted his head so that she could see the blue-gold glitter on his brow. Her eyes nearly blinded him but he forced his hand towards her until it touched her wing. The tips of his finger sizzled and burned. There was a flash and a burning ache along his arm into his brow-band. It shook him wide awake. He wanted to rub snow on the burns.

The Dream-Seller shouted a curse and the Firebirds opened their wings, covering him with golden light until he burrowed into the snow like a worm.

Gilen stroked the Firebird's feathers. 'We need your help. If you get us out of here, I'll never forget. Will you help us, Sun-Fire?'

The bird arched her neck and red sparks scattered between the golden flames. 'We'll stay with you as long as we can, but this place has weakened you. We're already cooler. Tell your friends to climb onto our backs. Our flames won't burn them.'

Gilen did not have to tell the other's anything, they had already scrambled up the birds' wings. They found hand-holds between the long feathers and the flames slid around them and did not burn them.

Zoo clambered up behind Gilen and the Scouran boy turned to smile at him. Zoo was shocked by his face.

'Zoo, I might fall off.' He swallowed and shivered. 'Don't let me fall asleep, Zoo. I have to keep the Betrayer away from us. He'll find me if I sleep . . . Mustn't sleep . . .'

Zoo wondered if Gilen was going silly with lack of sleep. It would be a good idea if he did rest.

'I won't let you fall,' Zoo said, and he grabbed a handful of Gilen's jacket. An angry mouse-nose appeared and two beady eyes glared up at him for squeezing it so tightly. Zoo was so embarrassed he found himself apologizing to a mouse.

The Firebird called Sun-Fire curled her claws and shook her wings over the snow. The light was blinding and Zoo flinched away. Then she tensed and jumped straight up into the air. Zoo said 'Weeeeoooowwwhhh!!' And they were flying over the frozen city, leaving the grey men and the river and the Dream-Seller's screaming fury far behind.

Zoo decided that he liked this sort of flying. The Firebird's back was warm and the feathers felt like real feathers even when they looked like flames. He watched the fire run up and down his legs. When he touched it, he could feel the plasticky quills and the smaller feathers, as soft as duck-down.

Zoo quietly opened a new brain-box and hoped Gilen was too tired to wake up. 'Where are we going?'

The bird glanced at him over her shoulder. 'I wondered when you'd start asking questions.' She cracked a rough laugh. 'Something in the City is eating the Prince's strength. We'll go far south to rest, then find you somewhere safe.' She flicked her wing tips at Zoo's back. 'Don't let him fall, fat boy.'

'I won't, I promise.' Zoo chewed his lip, wondering. 'Do you mind if I ask you something? If your feathers are really fire, don't they ever go out?'

The Firebird croaked and Zoo nearly overbalanced. 'Questions, questions. We borrow the fire from the sun. Where there's no sun, we lose the fire. That's the way the Old Storytellers made us. We can live forever or die on a cold night. The Scouran kings liked that. It reminded them that even the most powerful could flicker away. That's why their greatest leaders can call us, if they're worthy.'

Zoo thought about it. Even Wikkit listened, respectfully. 'Is Gilen worthy?'

The bird tossed her head. 'He is, he was and he always will be, if he can live through this fight. But if he doesn't live, Firebirds will never rob the sun again.'

DEEP COLD

Tod was in difficulties. Sheeni would not stop wriggling about. At first, the dog had yelped with fright and dug his claws into Tod's legs. Now, Sheeni enjoyed the rush of wind and the view over the frozen landscape. He pushed his head under Tod's arm, twisted right round to peer over his shoulder, licked him on the nose. His tail poked Tod in the eye and the tears ran down Tod's cold face.

'Sheeni! Snerd-brained . . . ! Stupid . . . ! Stop wriggling!'

Sheeni barked and licked his nose again.

They had been flying south for hours and the sun was setting. Red light settled in layers across the sky. Soon, it would be very cold indeed. As it got colder, the Firebirds lost their light. The gold faded away and the real feathers showed through. Dull, brown, ordinary feathers.

Tod was relieved when the birds started to sink earthwards and he watched the icy tops of trees blur below them. Tall, barbed-ice trees . . . With no one to cut them down, the trees had grown wild. Apart from the cities and scattered farming communities, the rest of the world had turned back into a woody wilderness. Wild animals might be hiding down there.

Tod was thinking about wolves and bears when

the birds came down in a small clearing. Stiff-legged, the friends slithered to the ground and rubbed their aching muscles. Zoo was stretching his back when he saw Gilen fall. The Scouran's thin body crumpled into the snow and lay there, not moving.

A forest of eyes had watched the birds land. The first of the squirrels hopped forwards before their long claws had met the ice. Shivering deer followed, picking a way over the snow on their tiny hooves. The forest creatures were in their summer coats and the cold had driven them together, just to share some body warmth. Most had their young with them and the fauns slithered on the ice and bleated until their mothers nuzzled their necks. Within seconds of the Firebirds arriving, they were surrounded by curious woodland animals.

The friends were in trouble. They had used too much energy at the river. Even Tessa had no healing power left. Sheeni started to cry and paw at Gilen's arm, trying to make him move again. Wikkit had struggled free and he sniffed at Gilen's face anxiously. Everyone could see that the Scouran boy was too blue-less and his skin was icy.

'Why won't he trust us?' Tod stamped his foot, shaking with anger and real worry. 'We should have done something together and now he's hurt himself. He's never looked this bad.'

One of the birds nudged Gilen's arm with its claws. 'He's lost all of his heat and we've none left to give him. You should build a fire.' It stopped and the feathers on its neck bristled. Its head suddenly jerked skywards. 'Listen! Deep Cold coming.'

The three birds turned to the north and flapped their wings, hissing. Zoo could hear the noise as well, but he did not recognize it. It was like someone unwrapping crackly paper but with strange, glassy, tingling sounds. He could imagine tiny glass bells.

The circle of animals scattered. Deer leapt between the trees and squirrels ran along the branches as if their lives depended on it.

Tod shuddered. 'Deep Cold. I don't like the sound of that.'

Sun-Fire twisted around. 'Your enemy's found you! He's sending Deep Cold to kill us all. You have to build a fire!'

All around them the trees were solid with grey ice. The forest had a strange beauty. Its silver trees glittered like broken glass against the whiteness of the snow . . . Snow, ice, frost. There was no dry wood to burn.. How could they make a fire without wood?

'We've got to do something! Let's make a tent of blankets and put our heat-packs around him.' Tod rubbed at the ache in his head. 'I don't understand it. How could the Betrayer find us . . . ? Zoo, make a snow-wall to stop the wind.'

They had four blankets and three heat-packs. While Zoo scraped snow into a wind-break, Tod and Tessa arranged the packs along Gilen's body. Luz tucked him into the blankets. They could feel the bitter cold approaching. For a moment they all stopped moving and just looked at each other. Sheeni barked and dived on top of the pile of blankets to give Gilen his own warmth as well.

Zoo sighed. 'It's no use. If it's this cold when the noise is miles away, it's going to be like the North Pole. A few heat-packs aren't going to help.'

'Well, what else can we do?' Luz started to tremble. 'We can't burn ice. Unless Tod could carry Gilen high enough up? It might save two of us, even if the others freeze.'

It was almost dark. The moon and the snow made a cold sort of light over the forest and there were no colours left. Even the orange inside Zoo's hood looked grey.

Zoo shook his head. 'No, Luz, high up would be even colder. And the cold might follow Tod up, just to get at Gilen.' Zoo thought hard. 'If we knew how long it was going to last, we could burn the blankets. Burn everything . . .'

But they had no idea how long the cold would last. Tessa had knelt to comfort Luz and Sheeni when she glanced over the trees. She shot upright, pointing. 'Look! It's falling on us!'

The Deep Cold was more than cold air. Above the wood, thousands of strands of ice tangled together and drifted down like a gigantic web. The brittle noise grew louder as it fell. Tessa put her hands over her ears as the ice-web crashed onto the tree-tops. Then they were trapped under it. The folds of ice slid between the trees and they were in a freezing tent, the cold driving towards them from all sides.

Zoo grabbed the ice pick and ran to the nearest lacy network of ice. He used all of his strength but the thin threads hardly moved. They fought back by blowing bitter cold into his face. The brown skin on his nose blistered and he stumbled backwards. Now he knew how snowmen felt. He groaned and looked up. And saw the insect.

Zoo screamed and dropped the pick. Staring down at him was a giant, grey-ice insect with crackling jaws, stalk eyes and jointed, freezing legs. Spines and scales prickled out of its shell and its claws were jagged pincers, just waiting to snap around a juicy snack. The insect clattered its mouth parts together and Zoo could see it thinking how tasty he would be. He screamed again, twisted and crashed straight into Tod, knocking him flat.

Luz had snatched the pick from the snow. She waved it at the insect, taking huge swings at its dangling legs. Tessa tried to roll Gilen over to get to his flares. They were in his pack, somewhere under the layer of blankets.

Tod pushed Zoo away and struggled to pull the big rope from his own pack. He had seen this ugly insect before. The cabbage wind had blown hundreds of them over the New Capital. They must have been very high up, to look so small. Tod's imagination had not pictured giant, flying insects. Just to have flying insects up there had been bad enough.

'I'll try to lassoo its legs.' He shivered and his teeth started to rattle. 'Come on, Zoo. Help the girls.'

Tod rushed forwards, ready for the fight. Behind him, his big friend shivered and closed his eyes.

Zoo could not move. He had never seen anything as ugly in his life. Ugly! He hated crawlies, hated them . . . And it was hungry. He recognized the hunger. He often felt like that when he was down to half a stomach. But he wasn't a gigantic insect with jaws as big as dinner plates. There was nothing in his brain-box to help with this feeling. It was pure, mindless panic and the boxes were numbed shut. Zoo sat on the floor, hugging his knees, and prayed that this was all a bad dream. He would wake up and be in his own bed with a snack-pack beside him and a new encyclopaedia to read. But he did not wake up. He screwed his eyes tight shut and moaned.

The insect dropped a steady flow of ice-web strands and they were incredibly sticky. Luz jumped backwards just in time. She watched the hard, scaly wings flutter on the insect's back and her skin crept. Only a Harg creature could be this repulsive. They were ugly on purpose, to terrify people. By the looks of Zoo, the idea was working.

'Go away!' She heard herself screaming at it. 'Leave us alone! Baghash ta Ohna!'

The insect rattled its legs along the web. Three long, two short, three long. A rest, then all over again. It tapped out a terrible rhythm. The noise seeped into heads and into frightened brains. Luz was sure she knew why but it was difficult to think. Then a sudden spurt and a circle of web caught the youngest Firebird around its neck. The bird squealed and clawed backwards, flapping and twisting to break free. Luz remembered. The beating sound was hypnotic. It slowed its victims and the poor bird was trapped, being dragged towards the hungry mouth.

Zoo heard Luz scream. He opened his eyes and saw the ugly ice-mouth dripping, waiting to bite into the beautiful bird.

Zoo choked, quivered all over . . . Ugly! Thing! He felt himself running and it was strange. His feet had never moved so fast. He felt odd inside. His mouth was open and he yelled a battlecry. Before he realized what was happening, he had both hands on the ice-web and was tearing at it furiously.

The web shivered once, then shattered earthwards. The insect crashed down in a tangle of broken threads and kicking, hairy legs. Zoo fell on it. He pounded at the creature's ice-body with his clenched fists and it started to splinter. Tiny cracks ran along its hairy-rough shell. Harder, hit it harder . . . He could feel the cracks growing. One more punch and the insect broke apart in a shower of ice-crystals. The cold light turned them into a diamond glitter, sparking a jagged trail over the snow. No insect left.

'Globby, horrible thing! Horrible, horrible . . . !' Zoo knew that everyone was staring at him. He snapped the ice-web strands from the Firebird's neck and stroked down the battered wing. The bird crackled and rubbed his chin with its closed beak in thanks. 'Now, let's have that fire!'

Zoo took hold of the nearest tree, tensed his

muscles and pulled. The tree snapped, half-way up its trunk. Inside was dry wood. As Zoo broke the trunk into rough planks, his friends came to squeeze his arm and give him silly, relieved grins. They all had their powers now. All except Gilen. They built a huge fire and drove the cold back towards the north. In the end, they heard the cold sigh in defeat. The last dripping pieces of ice-web vanished and the Betrayer had retreated.

* * *

The forest had never seen such a huge fire before. Flames shot into the darkness and the light drove the shadows deep into the trees. It melted the ice and the summer grass appeared underneath. Hungry deer pounced on the fresh green and the sound of chomping teeth filled the clearing. The Firebirds stood slightly apart from the others, stretching their wings to the fire to take some of its light.

Gilen sat very still, his face turned to the warmth. He had seen the Betrayer in a dream. The man had held out his hands and welcomed him but there had been hatred in the smiling eyes. Why would the man welcome him?

'I'm sorry, I shouldn't have fallen asleep. I couldn't help it, I was so weak . . .'

'Me too.' Luz coiled Wikkit's tail around her fingers. The mouse seemed to enjoy it. 'Maybe it's because he's so close to us. We're on the same world as him again. It was bad on Scouros, but it's worse here. Every time we get near to the City, we get weaker. It has to be one of his tricks for keeping us away from there.' Wikkit crawled up her sleeve and she shook him down again. 'If he's so desperate to keep us away from the Needle, there must be something about it that we can use against him.

113

Maybe it's got his heart inside and we just have to open it up, grab the heart and stamp on it.'

Gilen grinned at her. That was the sort of thing Luz would like to do. Nothing was ever that simple. A deer came to snuffle at his arm and he patted her and talked with her for a while. She told him how old and ill animals were suffering from cold and lack of food. Another few days and the whole forest would die. Even the trees were unprepared for ice. Their leaves should never have been green and open to the snow. All Gilen could do was promise to stop the cold, if he could.

'We have to go back to London.' He stood up and managed not to fall. 'Tomorrow's our birthday.' They had all forgotten and Gilen grimaced. 'I'm not sure why but I think we'll meet him tomorrow.'

Sun-Fire came to stand beside him and the weak gold of her new flames shone on his skin. 'We can't stay much longer. Don't try to hold us or you'll lose your strength. We can take you to the City, but then we have to go.' She stretched her wings and crackled at the sky. 'We'll try to find a safe place for you. We wish you well, little Prince.'

It was pitch-dark. There were no streetlights or fires or any sign of life as they flew away from the trees, back over the miles of empty countryside to frozen London. A thousand buildings lay beneath them and every one could be full of grey men and death.

The Firebirds circled over the city for a long time, just sensing the air and trying to find a friendly place to land. At last, they sank earthwards and Tod could make out a round shape, then two towers and a dark roof below. As they flew closer, he realized it was St Paul's Cathedral, glittering in its layer of ice. They were going to land on the balcony above the great dome.

Sun-Fire turned to look at the five pale faces. 'This is the safest place. I don't know why, but it still has a lot of goodness stored in the stone. It might hide you from the enemy's eyes for a while.'

'We're coming down on the Golden Gallery.' Gilen said. 'I remember from the history books. If we go inside the tower we can shelter for the night. I think we should stay near the top. Anyone coming after us will have to climb all the way up and that gives Tod time to fly the girls away.'

Luz was already lowering herself onto the slippery path and she glared back up at her brother. 'This time we'll stick together, no matter what. Promise me, Gilen.'

She put her feet squarely on the ice and fell over. While everyone helped her up, peered out at the view and said shaky goodbyes to the Firebirds, she had time to forget that he never did promise . . .

* * *

A pair of eagles lived at the top of the Telecom Tower. They had raised a nest of young that spring and they hunted over the whole city. That night, feathers fluffed out against the cold, they heard a voice calling them by name. They both flew north until they found the tall boy waiting for them above the cathedral dome. His eyes were silver and he could speak into their minds.

The eagles were wild and proud of their freedom. Their eyes were needle-sharp and could see a baby rabbit from high in the clouds. Their talons were iron-hard and could break bones. No one gave them orders, but this pale young-one was different. He asked them, as a lord would ask a trusted friend. They gave him their word to watch for his enemies and flew to their high nest like shadows on shadows.

Wikkit had not liked the eagles. He did not like

many things, not even his fellow mice. Gilen was used to his bad temper by now. They gazed out over the dark rooftops, Wikkit clinging onto the boy's shoulder.

'Mice here, low down.' The mouse twitched his whiskers towards the door. 'Fat cathedral mice. Not much use for fight 'less I give them talk-to.'

Gilen grinned at him. 'You want to use my thoughts to carry your voice to them? No swearing, then.'

Wikkit sniffed. His own mother had more than once nipped him behind the ear for strong language. He had been the fighter of the litter and she had been glad when he was big enough to fend for himself.

Gilen closed his eyes and let his mind become a loud-speaker to send Wikkit's squeaks to any mouse-brain in the cathedral. The poor creatures heard themselves called 'cowardly fat-gut churchers, eating kneeling-mats and old flags . . . better be ready tomorrow . . . or deal with Wikkit the Ear-Nip.' They squeaked back their promise to be as brave as any factory mouse. There was hurt pride at stake. Whoever tried to walk into St Paul's would find themselves in a mouse-war.

The pigeons had already heard about the Betrayer. A few had been with the ones Gilen had spoken to by the river. They had seen pig-men try to catch young fledgelings to eat and the whole pigeon population was alerted to watch for trouble.

'Well, if nothing else, we're going to be warned of any attack.' Gilen walked around the gallery, running his gloves along the iced rail. He could just see the top of the Needle between the ancient office blocks. 'Whatever happens, little friend, my Family Spirits will be proud of me. I won't let the Hargs see that I'm frightened.'

Wikkit crawled back into the warmth of Gilen's jacket. He scratched one ear and settled down for the night. 'If we had all factory mice . . .' He yawned, sleepily. 'You'd see, soft-skin. Pity only fat churchers.' And he fell asleep.

Zoo had forced the door to the Victoria Tower. Inside, a metal platform coated with ice led to a spiral staircase. Well wrapped up in their blankets, the four friends were already dozing. Luz just opened one eye when Gilen slid down next to her. Sheeni was his heat-pack and the dog's tail hit Luz on the shoulder a few times before Gilen calmed him down. Dog snores soon echoed through the tower. The whole City seemed to be asleep. Only Gilen sat with his eyes unblinking, staring down into the pitch darkness beyond the first flight of stairs and keeping watch for them all.

ST PAUL'S SURROUNDED

The grey men came an hour after daybreak. The eagles saw them walk over Blackfriars Bridge—stick-legged, pig-nosed, black-hatted. The Enemy. The eagles folded their wings and fell out of the sky, screeching.

Gilen stumbled to the rail above the dome and gazed over the rooftops. Wikkit clawed up his arm, squeaking. He had seen the eagles and he could smell the pig-men. The air turned bitter with cabbage-stink. What a birthday present!

'Wikkit, we've got to slow them down. Think the mice awake. Tell them to be careful.'

Mouse-squeaks filled St Paul's. Outside, the hawks swooped on the enemies, raking them with their claws. Their first dive took the Dream-Seller's hat and left him spitting curses.

Gilen called the pigeons. Their job was simple—pick up anything they could find and drop it. The grey men ducked and flinched as stones, lumps of ice and dead twigs rattled on their heads. Yellow Eyes was there, shaking with murder, and the Dream-Seller's eye-holes smiled as deep as wells.

Gilen ran into the tower. 'Wake up! They've found us.' He kicked Tod's legs. 'Tod, you've got to fly the girls to another roof.'

It had been a cold night. Their bones ached and

118

their muscles were stiff. Sheeni bounded to the rails, barking. The other pulled their back packs on and shuffled after him.

Zoo gazed over the edge of the dome. The pigeons were pooing on the pig-men. White blobs splattered every piggy face. 'Two hundred and thirty-nine of them.' He shuddered. 'Gilen, how did they find us?'

'I think they can find dreams.'

Silence. 'Find dreams . . . ?'

Tod exploded. 'You should have told us! We've all been dreaming away and you just let us!' He could hardly believe it. 'I bet you didn't sleep a wink!'

'Tod, I have to stay awake to keep your dreams safe from the Betrayer's creatures. While I was awake, they couldn't find us. But I was so tired . . . I couldn't stop the dreams escaping any more.'

Zoo groaned and hit himself on the forehead. 'Of course! That's what you meant when we were on the Firebirds! I should have guessed!'

Tod followed Gilen around the gallery, pink with anger. 'Then why didn't you wake us up and stop us dreaming . . . ? And why didn't you tell us, ages ago? We could have taken turns to keep you company. But you just let us dream away. You think you're the only one who can stay awake all night. You still don't trust us!'

Gilen turned so fast that Tod collided with him. The zips on their jackets clicked together. Ice surrounded them. Ice on the rail, ice on the tower above their heads, ice on the leaden dome. Ice in Gilen's eyes.

'I can't trust anyone! You haven't met him, Tod. He can offer you anything you want. No one can resist him. And I didn't wake you up because I fell asleep.' Gilen's lip suddenly quivered and he had to turn away. 'I fell asleep, Tod. When I woke up, it was too late, they were already here.'

Sometimes, Tod forgot that Gilen was only a boy, like himself. Well, not like himself. Gilen was Scouran and a prince, but he could still make mistakes and he could be hurt, just like anyone else. He looked hurt now, admitting that he had fallen asleep.

Tod's anger melted away. 'We can fight him if we stay together, Gilen.' He took a deep breath. 'I won't fly the girls off. We have to stay together. It's the only way we can beat the Betrayer, I just know it is.'

The others had followed and Luz put a hand on her brother's shoulder. 'Tod's right. We're too close to the Betrayer to be separated. If we split up, he'll just pick us off, one by one.'

'Then how do you suggest we get out of here?' Gilen pulled away from her. 'We're surrounded. We can't all fly.'

Tessa looked away. She wanted to cry very badly. Her eyes stung and she made them focus on the curve of icy dome. The shape make her think . . . Of a bridge! An ice bridge!

'Gilen! We'll build a bridge!'

Everyone stared at her.

'I know it sounds stupid but I'm sure we can do it. We just have to put our powers together, like Brother Gyus said. Luz can break the ice and Tod can fly it up to us. Then I'll try to heal it together. Zoo can give us his strength so that all of our powers are stronger. We can build a bridge right over to the Needle.'

'Good idea.' Gilen's face was strange. It should have warned them. 'You four stick together and build your bridge. I'll keep the grey men busy.' He dived through the door into the tower. The bolts slammed shut behind him.

Zoo kicked the wall, furious with himself. 'I'm working on one stomach, that's why I'm so stupid. I should have known he'd do that!'

120

Tod groaned. 'There's no time to argue with him. Tessa's right. We have to build a bridge. It's the only way to escape.'

* * *

The iron stairs were thick with ice. Gilen clung to the rail and took a step at a time. An icicle snapped and fell, shattering like breaking windows somewhere below. There was hardly any light but he did not dare use his torch, he needed both hands to hold the rail.

The iron stairs led to a door and outside, into the cold air. Gilen was below the dome now, and he snatched a glance over the stone wall. The grey men had vanished. They were inside, searching for a way up.

A narrow tunnel cut back through the wall and Gilen fell down it. His chin bounced off the stone and he bit the inside of this mouth. For a moment, he saw stars and tasted blood.

'S'all right, Wikkit . . . I'm OK.'

Water trickled between his fingers. Below him was a giant spiral of iced stone. Now, that would be quick! But how was he going to get back up it?

Gilen started to grin. 'Hang on, Wikkit.'

A push with his arms and he skidded onto the ice helter-skelter.

Square windows flashed past. Wooden seats . . . One rushed at him and he twisted to avoid it and lost his balance. Sliding backwards . . . The wall hit him on the shin and he winced and rolled over again. A blur of stone spiralled above him.

Gilen spun around the last bend. He was out of control. One leg kicked in the air, the other twisted under him, and then he saw the door. Gilen threw his arms over his face, just in time. Rusted hinges tore free and the door flew open. He crashed past it, hurting his knee . . . down a step, flat on his back . . . and catapulted into a mass of wrought-iron rails. There was an echoing crunch, then silence.

Whispering. Gilen opened his eyes and slid sideways onto the floor. There was blood on his face and he swung a hand up to find out why and hit himself on the nose. It hurt and he giggled.

He was still spinning. In front of him, the iron rails surrounded a huge, circular hole. Above the hole was the painted inside of the dome. Dazed, Gilen watched the moth-shapes of frozen prayers hover near the ceiling. Some prayers were too strong to fade away. He was in the Whispering Gallery and the whispers were closer.

Doors everywhere! Gilen staggered upright and grabbed the rail to stop himself falling. Doors opened all around the walls. Some would go up to the dome. The rest would go down. He looked over the rail.

A frozen cathedral—empty chairs, empty arches, rising pillars—all coated in ice. Frosty grass sprouted between the stones and small bushes grew out of the choir stalls. The mice had used the straw from the kneelers for their nests and birds had raised families around the walls.

St Paul's was full of stamping, arm-waving men. Several hundred mice and an angry flock of starlings were defending their home. Pig-feet stamped down on mouse-bodies, missed and skidded across the ice. The starlings flapped just out of reach, bombing the men with ice and frozen droppings. It was brave but it only slowed the men down. Some had already disappeared through a stone doorway.

Gilen shook his pack empty, then spread his jacket, orange side out, next to one of the doors leading to the top of the dome. He had his knife, some of Tod's ropes, the flares, an axe and his father's dart. He started to tie the flares to the iron railings.

Wikkit squeaked a warning. A door on the other side of the gallery slammed open, then the one right next to him. Gilen dived sideways, clawing at the nearest flare's pull-lighter. A tiny spark . . . The dome exploded into lime green fire and screams echoed around the walls. He had the next flare ready when he saw the Dream-Seller and the dark glasses over the man's hollow eyes. The forked tongue laughed.

'Clever! But once bitten, twice shy, Prince Gilen.' The Dream-Seller pushed a cringing grey man over the rail. 'Is that the best you can do? Pretty coloured lights?'

'Try this!'

Gilen grabbed the rope and pulled. All along the gallery, loops of slack rope tightened and jerked into the railings, pulling long legs with them. Half a dozen figures went over the rail. A few clung on. None of their friends took any notice. Gilen started to back towards his jacket.

The Dream-Seller raised one hand and everyone froze. 'Look at me.'

Gilen turned his head and stumbled for the door.

'Or are you afraid?' The Dream-Seller laughed. 'Are you afraid of me, Scouran? Are you only strong with all of your alien friends behind you?'

Gilen turned back, cold with anger. 'You aren't real,' he said. 'You're a rotten thought from his rotten head. Go back to him. GO!'

'GO.' The word drifted around the gallery and the Dream-Seller flinched. His smile vanished and he shook his head from side to side, shaking the word out of it.

'No, Prince. Not so easily.' He shook his head again, and his black tongue snaked out. 'No, you listen to me. Why don't you dream for a while? You're so tired! Don't you want to dream, little Prince?'

No! Gilen twisted away, but the voice was in his head. He was tired and cold. He needed the warmth of the jacket. Too late . . .

'Dream you're cold. You're cold to your heart, Scouran.' The whispers spread around the dome and back, sliding into Gilen's ears and into his head. 'Can't you feel the cold? It makes you tired, doesn't it? Sleep, then. Just lie down and sleep.'

The dome trapped all the sound in the cathedral. Mice and squawking starlings, grunting pig-men . . . And feet. Feet walking towards him on the ice.

Gilen was lying down. He was just too tired to fight any more. His head fell back onto the ice and it was so comfortable. He gazed at the painted figures on the ceiling. An old man with a beard was ordering younger men about, building something, somewhere, long ago.

'Help me . . .'

The old man looked down, frowning.

Gilen forced his voice to come. 'They're evil men. Please, help me. I can't move.'

The dome paintings were black and brown. Further down, coloured angels flew over the arches. Beautiful colours. Gilen's eyes fixed on the nearest angel and he thought the Old Words . . .

A pig-man raised one fist. The mouse squeaked at him and he snorted with laughter. As he brought his fist down, a brown and black, paper-thin hand took hold of it. Centuries-old paint wrapped around the piggy wrist. It had a nutcracker grip and pig-bones crumbled like burnt toast. The pig-man squealed with pain. A blue-winged angel swooped down, caught him by the bristles and neatly tossed him over the rail.

124

'No!!' The Dream-Seller screamed and lashed out with his fists. 'No! You can't do that! You aren't that strong!'

The painted faces kept the same serious expressions as they took the pig-men and threw them over the rail. The dome echoed with squeals and curses, thuds and breaking chairs, far below . . . Only the Dream-Seller was left and the faces drifted towards him. He backed away, cursing them, cursing everyone who had anything to do with this stupid fight. And then the faces stopped and started to curl at the edges. Slowly, they folded into flaking piles of paint.

The Dream-Seller threw his head back and howled with laughter. 'That's it, little Prince! You're finished. Sleep. Sleep forever.'

There was no more sound, just the dark, tired ache pulling him down. Gilen slipped away into darkness.

Wikkit felt his friend's body sleep. The lizard tongue was coming. Only one thing to do. Wikkit scrambled up the boy's neck and drove sharp, mouse teeth into the left earlobe.

Gilen yelled. That hurt! Blood burned down his neck. When he opened his eyes, tears spilled out and the Dream-Seller was next to him, reaching forward.

Wikkit leapt onto the man's hand and bit into the thumb. The Dream-Seller squealed and knocked him away. It brought Gilen back to life. He thought of power and pointed to the old, iced-up organ pipes below the gallery. There had to be some power left in him somewhere. His arm shook. He gritted his teeth and his shirt sleeves ripped up to the elbows. 'Play!' he was thinking. 'Play!'

The Dream-Seller's mouth twisted, his black nails curling to scratch the poisoned knife.

The frozen organ groaned. Ice creaked in the pipes. Another groan, louder, than a deafening howl of sound. The ice in the organ pipes shattered and St Paul's rocked with music. It knocked Gilen backwards. Every window in the dome exploded.

'Gilen, it's finished!' Tod's voice. 'Gilen, where are you?'

The Dream-Seller snarled and swung the knife. Gilen ducked under it. He grabbed Wikkit and threw himself along the ice just as Tod flew through a broken window.

'Gilen . . . ?'

'Tod! Here!' Gilen leapt onto the rail.

Tod saw him and dived. 'Jump, Gilen! Jump . . . ! I'll catch you.'

Gilen's legs tensed to jump and a hand grabbed him by the hair and snapped his head back. The Dream-Seller tore him away from the rail and he sprawled onto the floor. The breath choked out of him and he could see the poisoned knife coming and he was too shaken to move. Tod swooped across the dome and threw his back pack. It was heavy, full of metal and it knocked the Dream-Seller sideways. Then Gilen saw the knife turn to aim at Tod's chest.

'No! Tod, dive! Look out! Tod!!'

There was nowhere to dodge. The dome was a perfect trap and Tod was like a fish in a bucket. The Dream-Seller aimed, then hesitated. He turned and smiled at Gilen. 'You had to be together, Scouran. Now there'll be only four of you!'

The Scouran dart was in Gilen's hand. The Dream-Seller recognized it and his tongue flickered in disbelief. They both took aim. Gilem emptied his mind and the Old Words rang out of him. He had remembered words he had never heard. It was the Scouran way. His father would have been proud.

The dart struck the Dream-Seller in his empty heart. He frowned and looked down at the flights sticking out of his ribs. His eye-holes slid up and stared at the blue child who had done this. They could not believe it. A gurgling sound at the back of his throat, a splutter and twitch. The Dream-Seller's skin turned shiny black and his empty eyes closed. Then he vanished, just black water trickling over the ice.

Tod jumped over the rail and grabbed Gilen by the belt, hauling him into the air. The next wave of grey men arrived too late. The two boys were out through the window and in free air.

'You remembered the words, Gilen,' Tod panted. 'You saved my life.'

'And now you're saving mine.'

'Oh no!' Tod stopped, staring back through the broken window into the dome. 'Gilen, you've left the dart behind!'

'It's gone, Tod.' Gilen shivered. 'Once throw-darts are used, their power dies and they fade away.'

It had been their only weapon against the Betrayer. Tod stared at Gilen, horrified. 'Oh no!'

'Tod, it was worth losing the dart to save your life. I couldn't stand there and let him kill you.'

They were floating just under the golden gallery and Tod knew that his face was stupid with shock. 'But Gilen . . . ! If you haven't got the dart . . .' He shook his head, helplessly. 'What are you going to do?'

And Gilen suddenly laughed. It was a frightening, shaky laugh. It frightened Tod more than a whole universe full of pig-men. 'Tod, I just don't know.'

They were exhausted and Gilen was shivering, without his jacket. As the grey men slithered and fell up the frozen stairs, the friends roped themselves together and followed Sheeni onto the ice-bridge.

The bridge was as wide as a single bed and slightly thicker than a mattress. Luz had used her strength and Zoo's to break pieces of ice from the surrounding buildings. The rough, chunky blocks jutted in every direction. The whole thing had a dull sparkle like grubby diamonds.

As soon as they were out of the shelter of St Paul's, the breeze turned into a gusting monster doing its best to blow them away. It took all of their strength to stay on top and they had to bend forwards into the gale. Only Sheeni scrabbled ahead at speed and the dog's red ears flapped like flags. Red for danger. Grey clouds galloped over the sky from the north and the air quivered with cold.

'They aren't following.' Zoo stopped to peer over his shoulder. 'Look, they're just watching us. Why aren't they following us?'

'They don't have to, do they?' Gilen nodded towards the Grey Needle. 'We're going just where they want us to go.'

Everyone stared at him. Luz scowled, angrily. 'What do you mean, "where they want us to go"? I thought we were escaping.'

Gilen sighed. 'Haven't you guessed, yet? The Betrayer wants us exactly where we are. People always do what he wants. The Wise One knew we had to come to Earth because it has the number five over it. But the Betrayer knew about the five as well. The Hargs have been preparing the Earth for us, for centuries.'

Gilen rubbed his hands down his cold arms. His voice was hard and bitter. 'This is the last planet in the universe we should have come to. And the Needle is the most dangerous place on Earth for me. The Betrayer fooled us, just like he fooled my father. He made us think he didn't want us here. The harder he tried to keep us away, the harder he knew we'd fight to resist him. And it worked. We've walked right into his trap.'

'Why didn't you tell us!' Tod was furious. 'You should have told us.'

'I didn't know until last night. It's the Needle. I could only read some of the writing in the history video. It gave the dates that it was built and today's date and called them The Start and The Finish . . . It didn't make sense. Why would it say The Finish for our birthdays? But the closer we got to it, the weaker we were. When I finally saw it, I just knew.' Gilen looked down, for a moment, and his eyes were sad. Then he grinned. 'I didn't think you'd feel any better if I told you.'

Despite himself, Tod grinned back. 'You're snerd-brained, Gilen. Half snerd-brained.'

Gilen shrugged. 'Well, whatever. We had to come here or spend the rest of our lives running. I'd rather get it over with.'

Zoo took the strain at the top of the bridge and the others let themselves down the rope, slithering on the lumpy ice. Every tree and bush near the Needle had dried up. There was no life here, not a single rabbit-dropping on the snow.

Sheeni had fallen strangely silent and Tod bent down to stroke the dog's neck. He could feel the white fur starting to stand on end. Then he heard the voice.

'Now!' it said. 'Now, little Prince. Welcome to my world.'

129

GILEN AND THE BETRAYER

The dark wind took them by surprise and the world
turned black. Zoo fell the last few metres and
bounced onto the snow. The horrible smell of cabbage choked them and then grey men were everywhere. The Needle shuddered as if someone inside
was shaking himself awake.

The grey metal was colder than any ice. It was
pulling all the warmth from the world and eating it.
Tod's feet turned numb and he wobbled into Zoo.
Gilen was right, the Needle was taking their strength
away.

Yellow Eyes came first, grinning and showing his
teeth as he stepped out of thin air. Someone was
behind him. Tessa put her glove in her mouth to
stop a squawk of horror.

This was the Betrayer. His skin was thick, grey,
damp as a sponge. He looked like a mouldy wall
where the plaster was growing mushrooms. All of
his features seemed half-grown . . . tiny nose, tiny
mouth, tiny black eyes in the small head. Underneath, his body was a massive, wobbling jelly.

The Betrayer looked at them and his little mouth
opened in a silent laugh. They could see his grey
tongue shaking but no sound came out.

Gilen stood very tall and still, but he was afraid.
He did not want his friends to be hurt and the

Needle was already weakening them. Luz was nearly blue-less. One of his hands twitched up to stroke Wikkit and take some strength from the angry whiskers.

'Welcome, little Prince!' The Betrayer's lips smacked together and a dribble of saliva ran down his grey chin. 'We Hargs have waited 600 years for this. Kiss my feet!'

Wikkit squeaked a strong word and Gilen met the man's eyes. 'Let my friends go. Then kill me if you can.'

The Betrayer smiled. 'Freeze,' he said.

Tod gasped. His feet had frozen to the ice. He tried to turn around to see Zoo but his neck had locked inside. Only his eyes could move and they met Gilen's wide, brilliant silver ones. Gilen closed his eyes and Tod could move again. He heard Gilen's voice in his head saying, 'Hold hands.' They all heard it. They staggered together and grabbed each other's hands, a ring of four frightened faces shivering with the cold.

'Little alien fools! My people have planned this for generations! Do you think you can stop me?'

Gilen opened his eyes. He looked almost too tired to speak. 'We have to. You've broken all the Laws of Life. You Hargs have been killing an innocent world just to get at me. We have to stop you.'

This time, the silent laugh was shorter. There was a nasty twist in the Betrayer's mouth. Thin grey threads of power ran from the top of the Needle and into his back.

'You're right, of course. It's Harg poison-iron. It's been drinking the power from this world for 600 years, storing it up for me. It will help me to destroy you. And your little friends will help me, as well. All of your friends will help.'

The cabbage wind blew and it brought people with

131

it—and animals. Squeaking cathedral mice found themselves in the snow next to the two eagles and most of the pigeons in London. There was Zoo's dad, Mr Ku, and Miss Roberts, the history teacher; Brother Gyus and Guardian Beryn; and the Barrett family. Grandma Barrett said 'Nids' teeth!' because she had been knitting and had dropped a stitch.

Tod's dad looked at the Houses of Parliament and frowned. 'This looks like London. I think it is London.' His slippers were ankle-deep in snow and he opened his mouth for a hearty moan and saw his son and daughter and a lot of men who looked like pigs. 'I've got a Bad Feeling about this,' he said

Tessa burst into tears.

All of their friends were here, in the dark and the cold of the frozen Capital. All except the nids.

The Betrayer ran his eyes around the startled crowd and smiled. 'Now, Prince Gilen Erath. These people will help me to kill you.'

Tod saw the look on Gilen's face. It was not surprise. Gilen expected them to betray him, after all they had been through together! Tod was hurt and angry. 'No we won't! Gilen, that's what you're frightened of. Trusting us!'

The Betrayer laughed and walked forwards. The four friends gripped each other's hands tighter and waited. 'Tod Barrett,' he sneered. 'What do you want most in the world? To be tall! Wouldn't you like that, Tod? To be the tallest boy in your class? Think about it.'

The man walked closer, smiling, smiling. 'And little Tessa. Poor, plain little Tessa. Wouldn't you like to be pretty? I can make you pretty . . . And the Princess.' He gave Luz a mocking bow of the head. 'You could be Queen Luz Pelina Erath. I could let you rule Scouros. It's a little world, I don't need it. I can take everything else.'

'I don't want to be a Queen!' Luz yelled, then realized that it was a lie. Her face turned glassy-white with shock.

'Last of all, the Trimonese. Zoo, just imagine your very own university. Your pupils all looking up to you. I could show you all the wonders in the universe.' His mouth twisted. 'I could show you all the food in the universe. You could have a garden full of globerries and cream and pickled gurks. You must be so hungry!'

And his hand came out of a fold in his cloak holding the most green, the most juicy-crisp gurk that Zoo had ever seen. Zoo swallowed and felt his mouth watering.

'It doesn't matter.' Gilen's voice cut through them all like a needle of ice. 'You can't help it. I'm the only one he can't buy because the only thing I want will kill him. I won't blame you, Zoo.'

Zoo felt as if someone in lead boots had bounced on his stomachs. He spluttered and twitched his fingers. For the first time in his life, words failed him. His brain-boxes rattled uselessly. He saw tears run down Tessa's face and his whole plump body ached for a magic spell to change all of this. But there was no magic. His voice suddenly came out of his mouth in a howl of pure anger. His father stared at him as if he was a stranger.

'No! No, I'll never eat another gurk! Never, never, as long as I live!' Something clicked. Part of his brain opened and he saw everything . . . 'Gilen! Gilen, Tod's right!' It was all so clear. Zoo nearly jumped for joy. 'Don't you see? All you have to do is trust us just this once. He's frightened of you. He's got 600 years of the Earth's power but he still needs us to help kill you. He knows you can stop him. Trust us, Gilen. Just this once.'

133

Gilen shook his head. 'It's no good, Zoo. It doesn't work. I do trust you . . .'

Gilen stopped and they saw him stiffen and his eyes fly wide open. He had stopped breathing. His body could have been carved out of the snow. On his shoulder, Wikkit twittered with excitement, the electricity spiking his fur like a giant caterpillar.

Sheeni threw his head back and gave a weird howl. It made the whole circle of people and animals shiver. Even the pig-men . . . Even Yellow eyes . . . Everyone felt the howl deep inside them.

Zoo watched the familiar blue sparks crack between Gilen's fingers. This time, they spread along his wrists, up the white arms of his shirt and shattered in all directions. His knees shook and he wrapped his arms around his head, his whole body a cloud of exploding energy. Gilen's eyes squeezed tight shut. Tiny sparks danced on his lashes and along the blue-gold circle of his brow-band.

Something warm and furry hit Zoo on the nose. It was Wikkit. The mouse's tail shot straight up in the air and his whiskers curled like springs. Wild with excitement, he jumped into Zoo's bald head and squeaked his battlecry.

Gilen's arms fell to his sides. He took a long, slow breath and his body straightened out to standing. Then his eyes opened. Zoo swallowed a sudden lump in his throat. Gilen's eyes were as blue as the summer sky and the blue-gold band around his brow flared and dazzled.

Luz squealed. 'Gilen!' Her voice cracked and she had to turn away.

A new boy stood in the snow. Summer blue shone in his hair and in his eyes and in the gold around his brow. He seemed taller and stronger. He looked at the Betrayer and the big man stumbled backwards, hands clutched over his face in purest terror.

134

Gilen frowned at the clouds choking the sky. He pointed at them and the earth under his feet started to tremble. There was a feeling of pressure, a surge of some incredible energy and the clouds started to fray at the edges. They darkened and tightened and began to revolve, coiling and boiling.

Blue light ripped across the sky and a different wind swept the City. It was like fresh water, crystal light. It swung around St Paul's and along the frozen Thames, then it twisted over Big Ben and swept down on the Grey Needle. The Barrett family toppled like dominoes and frightened mice scuttled between the eagles' legs.

The wind threaded between Gilen's fingers and changed direction. It rose in a vertical column a million miles high and started to suck upwards. Tessa's plaits stood on end and she yelped, staring at the spinning mass of clouds. Going up . . . Up . . . Thinner. She felt the warmth on her face and golden, August sunshine streamed onto the snow.

'Tessa,' Gilen smiled at her. 'This is for you. Happy birthday.'

The ice bridge shivered and turned into a shining, triple rainbow from the dome of St Paul's Cathedral to the foot of the Grey Needle. Ruby and gold and emerald light turned the snow into a stained-glass window of colour. The bells in Big Ben started to ring. Every church bell in London was ringing!

The grey men screamed and threw themselves on the ground. Yellow Eyes crawled in circles, tearing at the snow for a hole to crawl into. The Betrayer trembled and whimpered. Behind him, the Grey Needle changed. Tod pulled his jacket off and jumped up and down, waving it around his head and laughing. His friend was still his friend. The new eyes might be blue, but there was the old Gilen in the wicked glitter. He was turning the grey metal to bright, glowing red.

Zoo howled with delight. 'Raspberry jelly! I can smell it!'

The Betrayer saw it and snarled like a dog. He had nowhere to go and the rainbow light covered him. His mouth twisted, gulping for air. His face was ugly with hatred and Zoo stopped laughing.

In the middle of all the colour and the mad bells and the sound of mice and flying pigeons, Gilen watched the man who had murdered his family. He pointed at the Betrayer's sweating face.

'Now I can see the words you left for me on the Needle . . . "Welcome to my world, last King of Scouros." You've been playing with us, like you've played with this planet.'

Gilen walked towards the quivering grey mass of his enemy and the man staggered and whimpered, trying to get away from the colours in the snow.

'My Family Spirits will never forgive you for killing my father and mother.' Gilen turned to his friends. 'And this planet will never forgive you, either. You don't deserve to breath its air.'

The Betrayer had nowhere else to walk. He squinted at Gilen from between his fingers, like some animal caught in a trap.

Gilen's blue eyes turned cold. 'Now, Shadrash the Betrayer, show us your real self.'

Real self . . . Real self . . . The words echoed over the melting snow. The Betrayer had no strength left and his creatures changed back to their own bodies. Tessa winced as the grey men became kicking, grey insects, each the size of a bucket-ball. Their stiff, hairy claws writhed and clattered. Yellow Eyes was a spider with a black body and evil, yellow spots. The Betrayer was more and more like the jelly behind him. His face was melting grey blancmange.

'You forgot to bring one group of our friends here, Betrayer. They should see your real face as well.'

Gilen kicked the ice and the ground split open. The next second, nids were everywhere. Bright-red, furry, tongues hanging out, eyes popping at the mound of raspberry jelly. The warm, grassy, hamstery smell covered the whole of Westminster.

There was nowhere to look without colour. Shadrash had to look Gilen full in the eyes and his powers died. His body puffed out and out, filled with air, inflated like a giant grey sausage. And popped. A rotting-cabbage smell gushed out and the wind sucked it up and then the grey insects followed, as easily as water down a drain. They all vanished upwards, crisping smaller until they burst into black flames and a trail of smoke.

Miss Roberts threw her hat into the air and cheered. Brother Gyus roared with laughter and swung Grandma Barrett off her feet, knitting flying. Guardian Beryn shook hands with Mr Ku. Mr and Mrs Barrett hugged each other and Tod was amazed to see his dad smiling.

'Gone,' Gilen said. Then he turned his back on everyone and started to shiver. Sheeni nuzzled his hand and the queen nid chewed at his trousers, anxiously.

'It's all right Gilen.' Tessa put her hand on his arm. 'They weren't real people, just bad air and smoke. They were his mind-creatures and he was worse than any of them. You didn't have to kill them in the end. They destroyed themselves because they couldn't look at you.'

Gilen turned back and his face was pale. 'I know. It's not that, Tessa. I nearly destroyed us as well. If Zoo hadn't yelled at me . . .'

Zoo turned a darker shade of chocolate. 'You just

137

had to say it out loud, that's all. You'd better take this mouse before it bites my eyebrows off.'

Wikkit jumped onto Gilen's shoulder. The new, blue eyes turned and found Tod.

'You told me as well, and I wouldn't listen. I'm sorry, Tod. I won't blame you if you don't forgive me. Are we still friends?'

Tod grinned. 'Course we are, snerd-brain.'

'I wish I could make you taller.'

Tod felt himself tingle inside and he turned beet-red. 'S'OK. I'd rather have you here.' He gulped a few times, then realized what the warm weight on his feet was. He was knee-deep in tongue-dripping nids. 'I think you'd better let the nids eat that jelly or they'll eat us!'

Zoo's stomachs groaned. 'Wait a bit. Couldn't I . . . ?'

'No. And no more pickled gurks, remember.' Gilen tried to look serious. 'If my ears didn't deceive me, you said you'd never eat another.'

Zoo's dad grinned at him, so he grinned back. No gurks! He looked at the hungry nids and cringed.

The queen nid sat up on her back legs and whiffled, asking Gilen's permission. He nodded and she launched herself. The whole crowd of nids leapt nose first into the pile of jelly. Red blobs spun through the air covering everything, dog and mice, eagles and Barretts, swooping seagulls and flapping pigeons. Zoo stood with his mouth open. The others moved back, giggling.

'So, there's only one thing left to do.' Gilen said.

They looked at each other. The rainbow light bathed the snow, everyone was smiling and all of the Betrayer's creatures had gone.

Luz frowned impatiently. 'Well, tell us, then. What now?'

'Honestly, Luz. You've got a memory like a

squeezed sponge. We wouldn't be here at all, if they hadn't helped us. It's cruel to leave them as a legend. They can help this world to grow again.'

He put his hands out, palms upwards, and they heard the distant rushing thunder. Rain? A storm? What, then?

Tessa twisted around. 'Look! Oh, look, so many of them!'

Firebirds in flight. They flew out of the sun, golden flames in their wings and tails and their eyes sunbright. They crackled and screamed out of the sky. Gilen had brought the whole flock and they started to fan their wings over the snow, the golden fire melting it and sending clouds of steam towards the Thames. All around the Houses of Parliament, blades of new grass pushed through the soil and the trees that had been dead for 600 years sprouted tiny leaves.

Covered in jelly and a happy smile, Zoo stood beside Tod and watched the birds flying overhead. They looked as delighted to be in a real sky as the girls were to wave up at them and feel their warmth.

Gilen was grinning wickedly. 'I've just had an idea,' he said.

Zoo rolled his eyes. 'Oh no. Please, don't tell me. I couldn't take it on two empty stomachs!'

'No, listen to me.' The grin widened and Gilen lowered his voice to a whisper. 'I was just thinking. What would Vinny say if he looked out of his window tomorrow morning and found it ten metres deep in raspberry jelly?'

There was a moment of contented silence as they all imagined the look on Vinny's face. Then Zoo frowned. 'I'd rather find mine full of pickled gurks.'

Gilen laughed. 'For the Scientific Advisor to the King of Scouros, nothing but the best. I want you all to help me be King. But not yet.' He smiled and let

Sheeni run off to lap up the final drips of jelly. 'First . . . first I think we should all have some excitement and adventure. How about it?'

The two friends watched the tall boy with the mouse on one shoulder walk away from them. When his back was to them, he was just like any tallish, bluish boy.

Tod glanced at Zoo, frowning. 'He could be joking,' he said. Then he grinned and ran to join the girls. 'But I don't think he is!'

Zoo carefully pulled a pickled gurk from his front pocket. He had promised. He sighed sadly, and gave it to a surprised nid. Then he cheered up. The universe had other tasty snacks. He might even find something better than a gurk. He ran to join the others and his head was full of dreams of adventure.